"I am not your enemy."

Lord Bancroft spoke in a smokey voice and his eyes smouldered. "But I promise you this, mam'selle, that one day soon we will become much much closer than friends."

Yvette's heart nearly stopped at the intensity of his voice. Before she could give him a proper set down, he kissed her softly on the mouth.

His voice caressed her. "There, you see, mam'selle? It's just as I said."

"You are despicable, Lord Bancroft," she countered. "A conniving, treacherous rakehell, and definitely not the gentleman you pretend to be."

"That does not signify," he answered, apparently unscathed. "What matters is that I always get what I want, and, mam'selle, I want *you*."

"There will be a snowstorm in July before I consent to be *your* doxy, my lord," she said as she swept imperiously from the room.

"Stranger things have happened, my dear," said Lord Bancroft softly. "Stranger things have happened."

THE LARK'S NEST

PHYLLIS TAYLOR PIANKA

Harlequin Books

TORONTO • NEW YORK • LONDON
AMSTERDAM • PARIS • SYDNEY • HAMBURG
STOCKHOLM • ATHENS • TOKYO • MILAN

To Ed, who makes my
heart sing

Published April 1991

ISBN 0-373-31148-6

THE LARK'S NEST

CHAPTER ONE

"THE COUNTESS is comin'! The countess is comin'. Aye, and she'll be 'ome tonight!" Millie Dawkins ran willy-nilly through the corridors of Berrington House to spread the word. Fredricks, the butler, looked down his nose at her complete lack of decorum and wrote in his little black book. Yvette Cordé, sitting for a moment with the housekeeper, Mrs. Grover, over a dish of tea, passed her a significant look. Fredricks was a high stickler for appearances. Millie was sure to hear about this infraction of rules, small though it was.

Fredricks grasped the lapels of his waistcoat. "You heard her, ladies. This is not the time to warm the seat of your chairs. Off with you now to your duties. Mrs. Grover, might I have a word with you about the dust on the chandelier in the salon?"

Mrs. Grover, his senior by several years, cast a quelling look at his retreating back as she picked up her cup and drained the last drop. "A word, 'e says. More likely a whole speech. Come, girl, you'd best get moving. You know you have to work twice as hard as the other girls to make up for the times you're off entertainin' the nobs."

"Yes, Mrs. Grover." Yvette smoothed her pearl grey uniform and adjusted the mob cap to contain the jet black curls which had escaped when she was dusting the carved balustrade on the grand staircase. "The party at Haverford Hall is tomorrow night, Mrs. Grover. I hope you haven't forgotten that I must practice my singing with Mr. Clarke tomorrow morning."

Mrs. Grover sighed. "That's the third party this month. Seems to me, miss, that you spend more time practicing your songs than you do on the dusting. 'Er ladyship may be after replacing you, should you so much as leave a smudge of dust on the wainscoting."

Yvette smiled. They both knew just how unlikely such a scolding was, for Lady Emily herself had been responsible for Yvette's sudden popularity. From the night her ladyship had first asked Yvette to sing at Lord Berrington's party, the girl's fame had spread like fire over a puddle of hot grease. Now there were not enough days in the week for her to meet the demands of the ladies of the ton, each of whom begged her to entertain for them.

But now, taking her tray of cleaning materials, she climbed the stairs to the next floor and began applying warmed oil to the candle drippings on a Queen Anne table. It was so comforting to know that the pile of gold coins hidden in the hat box in her armoire continued to grow at a rapid pace. It was more money than she had seen since...

She paused in midthought. The money was one thing, but the danger that she would one day be found out loomed like a threatening shadow over her. Someone would eventually look beyond the façade she wore and uncover the real Yvette Cordé, uncover the secret she had kept buried for all these years.

She rubbed away at the edges of the congealed wax with more than her usual vigour. If she had the least bit of sense she would have no more to do with the business of singing. But no, she couldn't: it was the only way she could store up some kind of security. Or rather, the only way short of becoming someone's mistress. Her mouth tightened. Heaven knew there were plenty of men willing enough to become her protector. There were even a few men, tradesmen and hucksters, who had offered marriage, but they held no appeal for her, save for her need for companionship. And nowadays she was too busy to be lonely.

She gave a final polish to the tabletop and scrambled to her feet when she saw Lady Emily coming down the corridor. It was little less than a year since Emily Harding, the impoverished widow of Henry Harding, Lord Wallingford, had arrived at Berrington House. She had overset the entire household when she had delivered the ragamuffin who claimed to be the earl's mother, to the house. The countess had been presumed lost at sea some eighteen years before. Although the earl originally insisted that the newcomer was an impostor, eventually he had come to accept her as part of the family. Certainly no outsider was bold enough to question them too closely about the truth of the matter. Whatever had taken place privately after her return, publicly Lady Margaret was welcomed with open arms. Even after her subsequent marriage to Mr. Harrington, a wealthy tradesman, she was still known to everyone as *the countess*.

Her daughter-in-law, Lady Emily, now mistress of the house, was over seven months with child. Yvette dropped a curtsy as her employer approached. "Are you all right, madam? Is there something I might get for you?"

Her golden hair tucked sedately under her cap, Emily leaned against the wall and heaved a sigh. "Thank you, Yvette, I only stopped for a moment to catch my breath. I'm afraid I climbed the stairs a little too quickly." She straightened and rubbed her back. "I trust you haven't forgotten that your pianist will be here in the morning to work on the music for the Wescott party tomorrow night.

It's sure to be an important occasion, considering it is to be held at Haverford Hall.''

"No, madam. I'm quite prepared. And the gold brocade gown we cut down and mended fits perfectly. I only wish you could be there with me. I feel much more confident when I can look out and see you in the audience.''

Emily adjusted the shawl against the afternoon chill. "I wish it too, Yvette, but I cannot risk my baby's health. Besides—'' she smiled mischievously ''—polite Society would never recover if I attended a soirée in my present condition.'' She carefully lowered herself down onto a bench beneath a tapestry of knights and their ladies dancing around a maypole in a wooded glen. Her blue wool dress spread out around her and she reached into a panier for a small box.

"I wonder, Yvette, if you would care to borrow a simple piece of jewellery to wear at the party?''

"Oh, your ladyship, I couldn't do that,'' she said as Emily lifted the lid to reveal a golden sapphire set in a circle of gold filigree suspended from a finely wrought chain. "It is *magnifique*. But what would his lordship say?''

"James has already given his blessing.'' Her eyes twinkled. "You will certainly want to look your best. I'm told that Lord Bancroft is among the invited guests.''

Yvette pulled a face. "Oh dear. His mother, the viscountess, will not like that. Her ladyship was most unhappy that her son brought me a cup of syllabub at the Vancostain ball four nights ago. Then he added to her displeasure by asking me to dance at the party earlier this week at Greenbrier Manor.'' Yvette looked down at the floor. "I could tell by the frown on her face that she thought servants should remain servants and not try to presume upon their betters.''

"Lady Bancroft is a prude, Yvette, as well as a snob. Indeed if truth be told, rumour has it that her own background is not all she pretends."

Lady Emily rose and steadied herself. "Wear the necklace, Yvette. It will not only paint a pleasing picture but it will make you feel like a princess. If you don't believe me, ask Lady Margaret when she returns in a few hours. She is a firm advocate of the positive benefit of wearing expensive jewellery."

"*Merci,* your ladyship. You are far too kind." She dropped a curtsy. "Will the countess and her new husband be staying long at Berrington House, your ladyship?"

"We hope to keep them here until after our baby is born but a great deal depends on Mr. Harrington and his work. Since he bought Cyrus Grimstead's dressmaking establishment, he and the countess have had little time to themselves. Even their trip to China following their marriage was for the purpose of buying silks for her new line of ball gowns."

"We are all aflutter waiting for her to return. Lady Margaret always makes us laugh. I hope she has not changed."

Emily chuckled. "If anyone could domesticate her, it would be Mr. Harrington, but I seriously doubt that even he could do the job. It would be like trying to tame a whirlwind.

"Oh!" She rested her hands on her protruding abdomen. "This baby is sure to be wearing Hessians when he's born. I think perhaps he's telling me it's time to take a nap."

Yvette thanked her again and tucked the boxed necklace into the pocket of her uniform. She could hardly wait to see how it would look next to the gold brocade ball gown, but a dark look from Fredricks, who had just started down the corridor, kept her from racing to the servants' quarters to try it on at once.

THE COUNTESS AND MR. HARRINGTON arrived by carriage just after seven that evening. For the first time in weeks, Berrington House came alive with unrestrained laughter from the cellars to the attic; the countess had that effect on its inhabitants. Even though she had married a commoner, the title was so much a part of her personality that it never occurred to anyone to refer to her as Mrs. Harrington.

Yvette had just finished setting the library to rights after the family had gathered for brandy and conversation when Lady Margaret, her grey curls framing her becomingly lined face, accosted her.

"Ah! There you are, my girl. I've been waiting to speak to you," she said, lifting her quizzing glass to her nose. "James tells me you've caused quite a commotion among the ton." Her eyes twinkled with merriment. "And they say that the Duke of York has been making enquiries about you. Next thing we know, 'twill be Prinny himself summoning you for an audience."

Yvette tensed. "The duke has been asking questions about me? What kind of questions, if I may be so bold, your ladyship?"

"Oh my, what have I said? I didn't mean to alarm you, child. I meant only that everyone has heard about you and wants you to sing at their parties." She adjusted her pearls, a gift from Lord Berrington, and settled herself into a deep chair. "Truly, my dear, isn't it time that you gave up this menial position and settled into a house of your own?"

"Oh, madam. *Je ne sais plus où j'en suis.*" She flushed. "Forgive me. What I mean to say is that I am all astray. I don't know what to do. I have indeed found it difficult of late to juggle both halves of my life." She spread her hands in despair. "Am I a maid or am I a *chanteuse?*"

The countess patted Yvette's shoulder. "Indeed, my dear. I know just what it means to be torn between two worlds. For your own peace of mind you must do something about it, and soon." She smiled. "You cannot be giving your full attention to either position if you go on like this."

"Oui." Yvette nodded. "I've known for some time that in fairness to Lady Emily, I must soon make a choice. Now that my popularity seems assured, I feel that I cannot refuse such an opportunity. So I've been saving my money with that thought in mind."

"There, you see. I knew you were a clever girl. Leave it to me, child. I'll have enquiries made and see if we can't find you a nice little house with a fashionable address."

"But a house is such a big step. I do not know that I have the courage to go out on my own."

"Nonsense, my dear. You have so much to bargain with. If I had your voice and your looks, I'd be the toast of Europe." Her mouth took on a merry slant. "As it is, my talents lie elsewhere." She pushed herself up from the chair, settled her fichu across her bosom and winked. "And speaking of that, Mr. Harrington is awaiting me in the library. The dear man enjoys a mild flirtation with his glass of sherry. We shall discuss this further."

Yvette tried unsuccessfully to keep from laughing. No, marriage hadn't changed Lady Margaret. She was still outspoken, still ready to take charge in her own inimitable way. But best of all, she radiated surprising happiness and good health for one who was already far beyond the age of flirtation.

IT WAS AT THE WESCOTT PARTY the following night that Yvette had another chance to speak to the countess. Much to Yvette's surprise, the carriage sent to fetch her to the party had arrived with Lord Wescott himself ensconced in the passenger seat across from her. His behaviour, though prudent, left no doubt in her mind that he was not immune to her feminine charms. She managed, just barely, to blunt his pointed suggestions with laughter and an eyebrow raised in the direction of Reginald Clarke, her pianist, who sat across from her on the far side of the carriage, a model of discretion.

Because Yvette lacked the services of a chaperon, Mr. Clarke also served as a sort of guardian whenever it became necessary. His skinny frame and bespectacled appearance belied a determination that few dared to oppose. Now he scowled darkly as the marquess handed her down from the carriage.

Nevertheless, his lordship spoke boldly. "Remember, mademoiselle. I claim the first dance."

"Surely you must know, my lord," Yvette replied, "that it is not fitting for me to join in the festivities. I am here only to sing." She carefully withdrew her hand and adjusted her skirt.

His voice was sharp-edged in contrast to his smile. "I recall, mademoiselle, that you danced with Lord Bancroft at the Vancostain ball a few nights ago."

"Lord Bancroft was very insistent."

"As I shall be." He retrieved her hand and kissed it as the footmen assembled to usher the trio into the house.

Haverford Hall sparkled with a thousand candles in a thousand, flower-encircled crystal goblets tucked into windowsills and niches and gracing tables set between gilded chairs in the magnificent ballroom. Nearly three hundred people milled about, sipping claret and nibbling from trays of apricot tarts or other sweetmeats tendered by servants in black-and-silver livery.

On a raised dais at the far end of the room, a string quartet played while a group of dancers executed the intricate patterns of a Cavendish quadrille.

Yvette felt a surge of excitement race through her. It wasn't just the anticipation of performing before this large assembly, although there was always an element of unreality about that. Rather, it was the thought of seeing Andrew Waverly, Viscount Bancroft. He was sure to be there. And he was sure to confront her. She only hoped that it would be after she sang. He disturbed her in a most unsettling way. Where most men flirted outrageously, Lord Bancroft alternately praised then nettled her, a tactic which constantly kept her on guard.

Nevertheless, she searched the room for a glimpse of him. She was watching the Duke of Heatherfield execute a graceful turn with his lady when someone tapped her shoulder.

"Oh! 'Tis you, Lord Bancroft. I might have known," she said, taking in the satin breeches and the finely tailored coat which set off his broad shoulders to perfection. Meeting his gaze, she was once again impressed by the intensity with which he studied her.

He bowed. "Am I to assume you were expecting me? If so, mademoiselle, I take even greater pleasure in the knowledge that you are here."

"Take care not to assume too much, Lord Bancroft. It has been said that one cannot measure the rainfall simply by looking at the clouds."

"Quite so. Does that mean that you predict stormy weather ahead?"

"Certainly not. I try never to anticipate the future."

"How insufferably dull. To me the past is nothing. The present depends entirely on the company at hand, and the future is both a challenge and a goal."

A smile curved her mouth. "And just what is your goal, if I may be so bold?"

His eyes darkened to the colour of deep, blue water. "I think for the present our personal goals should remain our own. In time you shall know. Besides, an ounce of surprise equals a ton of spice, don't you agree?"

"Perhaps that is true, but everyone knows that too much spice can spoil the pudding." Yvette could not resist the challenge to match wits with him.

"Ah, there you have it. Though it's not pudding I have on my agenda, but a recipe far more exotic than you could ever imagine."

Yvette rolled her eyes in mock panic. "*Pas possible! Dare I ask?*"

He crossed his arms and tapped his fingers against his coat sleeves as he studied her face and pondered his response. This was no shrinking violet. This woman was unlike the spoiled débutantes with whom he dallied more often than not. Yvette Cordé had a voice to shame a nightingale and a face and form to woo the gods. She wore her courage like a suit of armour, yet underneath that veneer he sensed a spirit as adventurous and as passionate as his own. And by the gods, he intended to best her.

Yvette playfully peered at Lord Bancroft in an effort to recapture his attention. "I am waiting, my lord. Just what is this culinary delight that defies description?"

"Did I say culinary? Be careful, my girl. For now it is you who are assuming too much." He touched his forehead in mock salute. "May I change the subject to say how delightful it is that you have finally arrived? The party has not begun until this moment."

"My lord, you are too kind." She dropped a curtsy. "I have come at the appointed time. Was it your impression I was to arrive before now?"

"You have missed most of the dancing," he said, pushing back a lock of unruly brown hair with the palm of his hand.

"I am here to entertain, not to be entertained."

"Rubbish. You are as much a guest as anyone here."

"We both know that is not true." Yvette lifted her chin and regarded him steadily.

"Then I shall see that it becomes so. The musicians are about to finish the quadrille. A gavotte is sure to be next. May I have the pleasure of dancing it with you?"

Yvette was much tempted, but she could not afford to make enemies. Andrew's mother, the viscountess, was as watchful as the dragon who guarded the gold apples of Hesperides, when it came to her son's companions. Even now she was viewing the couple from the far end of the room, lorgnette pressed tightly against her eyes.

Yvette passed her fan in front of her face and tilted her head. "Thank you, Lord Bancroft, but I fear I must decline."

She started to turn away but he grasped her wrist. "You might as well consent, mademoiselle. I am not a cloddish yokel to be turned away with the flick of a fan."

She looked pointedly at the hand that held her wrist. "Neither are you the gentleman I thought you to be. Kindly unhand me, sir. You are making a spectacle of yourself."

He straightened. "Forgive me. I ask again, mademoiselle. May I have the pleasure of the next waltz?"

Yvette saw with mixed gratitude that the musicians were gathering up their music. She gestured toward her hostess, who stood gazing out over the crush of people. "I fear the answer remains the same, Lord Bancroft. I see that the musicians have retired for the nonce and it is time for me to sing. If you will excuse me, sir.'' She nodded coolly as she made to move away.

Andrew smiled at the setback but though his eyes signalled a look between promise and threat, his voice was soft as warm honey. ''Be assured that I haven't finished with you yet, Mademoiselle Cordé. Remember, the next waltz is mine.''

Yvette couldn't restrain the laughter which insisted on bubbling up whenever they had one of their confrontations. It ended quickly, however, when she saw Lady Bancroft cleaving her way through the crowd of merrymakers. Andrew swore under his breath and Yvette took the opportunity to slip away to the front of the room. Andrew was more than a match for his mother but if Yvette felt a twinge of guilt at leaving him to face her, it was soothed by a glorious sense of revenge.

Mr. Reginald Clarke had already taken his position at the piano. A muted rumble of conversation still echoed throughout the galleried walls of the ballroom and Lady Wescott expressed her concern that she could not quiet the crowd long enough to introduce Yvette.

Mr. Clarke lifted the lid of the piano. ''I think you need not concern yourself, your ladyship,'' he said, running his fingers over the keys of the newly acquired William Stodart. ''This piano is a full-bodied instrument compared to the harpsichord. Allow me to preface your words with a short, musical introduction.''

She nodded, then clasped her hands together and rested an elbow against the satin-smooth inlaid mahogany. It occurred to Yvette where she waited somewhat awkwardly in a chair, that nervous as she was before her performance, Lady Wescott was even more unsettled.

As Mr. Clarke predicted, the opening strains from a currently popular Ballad Opera, caught the attention of the audience and a wave of silence rolled from the front to the back of the room. Yvette was amused to see that even Lady Bancroft had elected to close her mouth for once and seek the comfort of a chair at the edge of the ballroom. Andrew appeared unscathed by the encounter with his mother and surprisingly, he had yet to seek the attention of one of the dozens of débutantes among whom he often held court. He was a handsome man with his square jaw, firm chin and finely chiselled mouth. If his dark hair was sometimes unruly, she laid that to the fact that it was abundant as well as scrupulously groomed.

Once quiet was established, Mr. Clarke allowed the music to fade away. He nodded to Lady Wescott, who moved with practised ease in her elaborate costume, to centre stage. She lifted her ample bosom then slowly expelled her breath, causing her heavy necklace of diamonds and rubies to glitter excessively.

"My dear friends. It has been more years than I care to admit since Haverford Hall has been graced by such a wealth of visitors. I must first thank each one of you for your cordial presence. Then, having said that, I shall introduce the charming young woman who is the reason most of you have come here tonight. Ladies, gentlemen, I present Mademoiselle Yvette Cordé. She will first perform 'A Tranquil Stroll in the Garden,' followed by the lively 'Shepherdess on the Green' and one of my own favourites, 'Ye Jolly Saints and Sinners.'"

A ripple of applause brought Yvette to her feet. She curtsied to Lady Westcott and took her place next to the piano. Mr. Clarke lifted an eyebrow, his gentle way of reminding Yvette to smile and stand tall, then began the opening bars of the first ballad.

From his place in the audience, Andrew, Lord Bancroft, stood tensely. He wanted Yvette to succeed, not only from pure selfishness, though to add her to his list of conquests would be a *coup de grâce* for even the most eligible of bachelors. But he had to admire her pluck: it was unheard of for a domestic of dubious parentage to rise to such heights. Seeing her standing like a queen on the dais above them, so beautiful, so proud, so much in command, he knew that her popularity was just beginning. He chuckled. So was his campaign to woo her. His best bay mare hung on the outcome of that wager, but wasn't there perhaps something more . . . ? Impatiently he scowled. He must not let the girl or the music distract him.

His gaze commanded her to look his way. Slowly, as if drawn by an invisible cord, her head turned towards him and their eyes met. Although she missed not a note or a word of the song she was singing, he knew by the way her eyes widened that she was under his spell. The knowledge thrilled him, but at the same time an inexplicable sliver of apprehension pierced the armour of his self-confidence.

Andrew forced himself to relax. No, by God. He had no reason for apprehension. He always treated his petticoats fairly and only kept one at a time. By accepting him as a protector she had little to lose. And considering her present lot in life, she had doubtless lost *that* several years ago.

Ah, but what a glorious voice the chit had. It was no wonder she had charmed the haut ton. Her songs went to the very core of his being like fine wine served in a crystal goblet, or memories conjured from a childhood fantasy. So deep within his thoughts was he that he had no idea the music had ended until the applause rocked the room with waves of "encore, encore." Yvette curtsied deeply and started to walk away but turned at last and spoke to her pianist. Then, raising her hand, she quieted the audience with a single gesture.

When she spoke, her voice was tremulous at first but her confidence grew with each word. "*Merci*. Thank you. You are most kind. I shall sing for you a French song I learned as a small girl in the village of Lyons."

She continued to speak but someone grasped Andrew's sleeve and he looked down at Mrs. Harrington, or "the countess" as she was known amongst the ton. He hardly knew the woman but he was aware that, despite the fact that Yvette was a mere servant, the Carstairs and the Harringtons took a proprietary care of her. He tried to ignore Lady Margaret but she plucked at his jacket.

"Lord Bancroft. If you please," the woman whispered behind her fan. "I wonder if I might have a word with you concerning our young friend?"

He blanched. *God's blood*. First his mother and now this feisty dragon was about to put her oar in. He frowned. "Can it not wait until after the programme is over, madam?"

"I fear the matter in question is most urgent, my lord."

"Very well, madam. If you insist."

She led him to a small alcove off to the side of the ballroom and he prepared himself for the worst.

Yvette had a momentary lapse of attention when she saw the two of them disappear from the main ballroom. Although she continued to sing without missing a beat, it was as if she were apart from herself, watching from a distance everything that was going on in the room. It was often that way when she sang. One part of her was the singer, the Lark from Lyons, as they had begun to call her. The other part was the watcher, the one who scanned the faces of the crowd. For in her heart she knew as surely as each dawn brought the sunrise, that one day someone from the past would see her and call her by name. And when that happened she would once again have to disappear.

One encore led to another until from sheer exhaustion Yvette had to refuse. Lady Wescott looked radiant. "What a success my party has turned out to be. It will be the talk of the ton. Surely, Yvette, you can find it in your heart to sing just one more song?"

Mr. Clarke left the piano and approached. "We must offer our regrets, madam, but the agreement was for three songs. We have already performed far beyond our limit. Mademoiselle Cordé is fatigued."

"Indeed! Well, I suppose if you refuse... I'm sure..."

She was interrupted by a group of Society ladies who surrounded them. Before Yvette could acknowledge the compliments, she was deluged with requests to entertain at other parties. Seeing that she was overwhelmed, Mr. Clarke took charge by saying that she must consult her schedule before she could commit herself to other engagements. Then the string quartet returned from their respite and the crowd was forced to leave the dais.

It was Lady Margaret who rescued Yvette from the throng of admirers. "Come, let us slip into the corridor. It leads to a small sitting room." She picked up a candlestick from a table, pushed open the door and closed it quietly behind them.

Yvette took in the dingy surroundings in one glance. "Oh, *mon Dieu!* Perhaps we should not be in here. This room isn't intended for company."

"Of course not, my dear. Why else would I have chosen it? The guest rooms are packed like peas in a pod." She put the candlestick down on a pedestal table that had long since lost its veneer. "Don't bother to sit. I hate to think what those chairs could do to our gowns. Now then," she said, reaching into her beaded reticule which was twin to the beading on the bodice of her grey velvet gown. "Lady Wescott asked me to give you your payment for entertaining tonight. Count it, my dear. Surely this can't be the right amount?"

Yvette laughed. "You've counted it already?"

"Yes, of course. I had my reasons."

Yvette spread some of the coins on her hand and counted the few remaining in the bag. "This is the correct amount. It's what we agreed upon. Mr. Clarke is always paid separately."

"Just as I thought. My dear, listen to me. Accept no more engagements until we've had a chance to sort this out. This is outrageous. They are treating you no better than a servant."

Yvette laughed. "But I *am* a servant. This is more money than I..."

"No." The countess was decisive. "I'll hear no more about it tonight. We shall talk tomorrow." She started towards the door, then turned back. "I told Lady Wescott that Mr. Harrington and I would see you home. We shall be ready to leave in exactly thirty minutes. Oh, yes. And tomorrow you and I are going to see a house that is for sale."

"A house! Oh, but I can't afford it."

"My dear child, you can't afford not to," she said as she swept out of the room.

Yvette followed close behind in a state just short of bewilderment. When they returned to the ballroom it was as if Lord Bancroft was expecting them. He stood next to a granite urn that, tall as he was, nearly dwarfed him. He gave a low bow.

"Mademoiselle. I believe the next dance is ours."

CHAPTER TWO

BEFORE SHE COULD REFUSE, Andrew signalled to the musicians and they began to play the "Lovers' Waltz." He took her hand and she resisted just long enough for him to register surprise.

"You aren't going to say no, are you, mademoiselle?"

Seeing the envy on the faces of several prim little débutantes in their white dresses and carefully dressed hair, Yvette felt justified. At the moment she wanted more than anything in the world to float around the ballroom on the arm of this dashing rake. Why should she deny herself, simply because such pleasures were considered beyond her present station in life?

She lowered her lashes then fluttered a look into his eyes. "Refuse you, my lord? I have been told that no one ever refuses you anything."

He laughed so boldly that other heads turned in their direction. "Precisely, mademoiselle. I trust I won't have to remind you of that in the future."

He whirled her into his arms and, holding her at a distance calculated to please even the most strait-laced dowager, waltzed her into the middle of the ballroom floor. Only a few dancers participated in the waltz, which was still too risqué for the tastes of the older party-goers. Yvette silently thanked Princess Lieven. The beautiful Russian noblewoman, known for her outrageous pranks, had been among the first to introduce the waltz to London Society. She had then brought it to Berrington House during one of the hat-making parties a year ago. The servants, as always invisible to their employers, had managed to learn the steps by watching the ladies frolic together.

Although this was the second time she had waltzed in public, Yvette had long ago lost count of the number of times she had danced with Millie Dawkins in the cavernous kitchen of Berrington House. And then there was the time on St. Martin's Day when Fredricks had downed one too many brandies in celebration of the firing of the fenny poppers. The staid butler had most uncharacteristically joined in the frivolities and danced more than once to the seductive strains of the "Lovers' Waltz."

And seductive it was, Yvette mused. Andrew was wise enough to maintain a respectful arm's length between them, thanks to the mob of watchers who were only too eager to spread the latest *on dit*. Instinct told her that, had circumstances been different, he would have held her against him until they moved as if joined together as one. The thought caused her foot to slip and Andrew tightened his hand on her back.

"Sorry," she murmured.

"Never apologize, mademoiselle. You dance like a wraith in my arms."

She smiled and looked up at him. "You are too kind, Lord Bancroft, but like a wraith, I must soon disappear. Lady Margaret and Mr. Harrington are waiting to escort me home."

"Will you grant me that pleasure?"

"Unchaperoned?" she asked without thinking. "Oh, I couldn't allow that! We both know that it would cause tongues to wag."

He executed a complicated turn before he responded. "When did you begin to worry about gossip? It isn't as if you were a pampered débutante, for whom Society decrees a dragon at every turn."

Yvette stopped dead on the floor and he caught himself in time before he fell over her. She glared at him. "*Mon Dieu!* Does that give you the right to treat me with less respect?"

His hands were becoming moist. "Forgive me. I didn't mean it that way. Shall we resume our dance before we create a scene?"

She went stiffly into his arms and he once again picked up the rhythm. It amazed Andrew that her eyes could go from warm to cold in less than an instant. He was determined to soothe her. "Ah, that is better. I meant no disrespect *chère mademoiselle*. I value your friendship too much to insult you."

"Then I suggest you stop rubbing your thumb over the palm of my hand." The voice was as glacial as the eyes.

He swore softly. "I apologize once again. It was a purely unconscious gesture. When I spoke a moment ago I only meant that a woman such as yourself need not be confined by the silly rules which govern a débutante's entrance into Society. You've no need to court favour. You are already more popular than the best the Season has to offer."

"If you believe that, sir, you are indeed blind. I am no more popular than a prized butler or a favoured chef. I am still a servant and you would be well advised to seek your pleasures elsewhere."

"We shall see," he said, turning his crooked smile on her face. Then he groaned. "I fear the dance is over before it has begun." He bowed. "It is only out of respect for your desire to avoid gossip that I decline to beg the next

dance. And I see that the countess is approaching. Thank
you, mademoiselle. I shall see you tomorrow."

She curtsied. "I admit to having enjoyed our waltz,
Lord Bancroft; however, I regret that our meeting tomorrow is out of the question."

"We shall see." He handed her over to the countess,
bowed and walked away.

There was something about his posture which reminded
Yvette of a cock in a hen-house. He was altogether too sure
of himself. *Mon Dieu,* she thought. There is something
about that man. He has a way with women. If it weren't
for that confounded English accent, Andrew, Lord Bancroft, could have passed for a Frenchman.

Lady Margaret chuckled. "Arrogant, isn't he? The
young cock of the walk reminds me a bit of James when he
was a boy."

Yvette looked surprised. "Lord Berrington? Oh, my
lady, I find it hard to imagine that he could ever have been
so brash."

"Brash and bold as a goose in the granary. It took a
good woman to smooth the rough edges, my dear."

"Lady Emily?"

"The same. And look at them now. A happy pair they
are." She slanted a look from behind her fan. "You could
work the same magic on Lord Bancroft, if you were so inclined," she said as she steered them towards the cloak-
room.

Yvette felt the heat rise in her face. "Surely you jest.
Have you forgotten that I am a servant, an upstairs maid,
no less? Lord Bancroft would never consider offering for
me. I have little to offer a man of his rank and title. Not
even a respectable dowry."

"Be that as it may. Andrew Waverly would provide well
for you, you may be sure of that. It isn't easy surviving on

your own, as we both well know. Sometimes one must make what one can out of what is available."

Yvette flushed scarlet but she had no chance to respond as they were joined by Mr. Harrington and a footman bearing their wraps.

Mr. Harrington beamed. "Mademoiselle. Your voice is a gift from the angels. I have heard many singers in my lifetime, the great Catalani included, but I have never been so moved."

Yvette shook her head. "To be compared to such a prima donna is more than one could hope for in a lifetime of performing."

His bushy eyebrows which, like his hair, appeared to be touched by an early frost, rose dramatically. "Mademoiselle, I predict that before the year is out you will have become the toast of London. Your name and your face will be known across the Continent and empires will fall at your feet."

The thought sobered her. "You are far too kind," she murmured.

The countess, seeing Yvette's obvious discomfort, motioned to her husband. "The footman is holding our wraps, my dear, and the driver will be waiting under the *porte-cochère*. Come. We have much to consider before tomorrow noon."

Mr. Harrington allowed himself to be helped into his many-caped cloak. "I'm sorry, Margaret, my sweet. Tomorrow I have a meeting with my solicitor."

The countess patted his arm. "This need not concern you, my love. Tomorrow Yvette is going to buy a house."

Of the two of them, Yvette knew she looked more astounded than Mr. Harrington. Having come from a humble background he had worked himself up to a position of social prominence, so it would come as no surprise to him that women sometimes had to do for themselves. She, however, was not so sure that she was ready to cut the pie.

She forced herself to remain silent while Lady Margaret was assisted into her ermine-trimmed cape. Her gaze roamed the room until it landed on the one man who stood head and shoulders above the crowd: Lord Bancroft. As was to be expected, he was surrounded by a gaggle of débutantes clacking and gabbling like so many geese in a fattening pen. He lifted his head for a moment and his gaze met hers. Even from across the room, even as she stood on the entrance staircase, she could feel his unspoken challenge.

And then her gaze was drawn some distance away to the left. Alicia, Viscountess Bancroft, stared at her with unblinking contempt. Her dark hair was wrapped in a braid that wound several times around her head. The effect aimed at was regal but to Yvette the ebony coils were sinister in the extreme. She was sorely tempted to throw her the witches' curse, a gesture she had learned as a child, but good sense reigned and she sent instead a bewitching smile. Lady Bancroft seemed to pale a little, then she lifted her chin and turned her back. None too soon, the countess reminded Yvette that the carriage was waiting at the door.

THE FOLLOWING MORNING, Yvette was interrupted in her musings by Fredricks. His voice was drier than usual as he said, "If mademoiselle could manage to tear herself away from her work, her ladyship wishes to speak with her in the breakfast room."

Yvette looked down at the Venetian tiles on the fireplace, which she should have been cleaning. "I still haven't finished..."

"Finished? Finished, you say? It appears to me you have yet to begin." He made an obvious effort to conceal his outrage. "Go...go before I speak my mind."

Yvette got up from her place on the floor and brushed at her uniform. "I'm sorry, I..." He walked away before she had time to apologize fully.

There was no need to change her apron before her audience with Lady Emily. She realized with chagrin that she had not completed enough work to soil it. The countess was right; something had to be done. She was no longer doing justice to her duties in the Berrington household. The time had come for her to choose between being a servant and a Society singer. It would not be an easy choice, but the reason for her reluctance must ever remain her secret.

As it turned out, Yvette had no need to make a decision or provide an explanation. Lady Margaret had already paved the way. Lady Emily, gracious as always, let it be known that she cared for Yvette as much as if she had been with the family for generations. But she also understood that Yvette must seize each opportunity to better herself. To do so meant keeping her own household.

Yvette felt a rush of fear, which was somewhat diluted by the countess who said, "Take courage, my girl. The worst that can happen to you is that you fail. In that event, suffice it to say, you can always return to Berrington House or to my own establishment once Mr. Harrington and I are settled."

Yvette looked up from lowered lashes, a slow smile curving her mouth. "I doubt very much that Fredricks would agree to my returning here, your ladyship, but the offer is reassuring."

They joined in laughter, and when it was over, they agreed that as soon as Yvette was established in her own home, her employment at Berrington House would cease. In the meantime, Lady Emily would see to it that her duties were merely token, in order to give her time to make the transition.

The countess was jubilant. "Now run to your room, my girl, and put on something suitable. Your brown wool with the ivory fichu, I think. I'm dying to have a look at this house in St. John's Wood."

Yvette stopped dead in her tracks. "*Mon Dieu!* You might as well have said Mayfair. I could not afford such a place."

"Nonsense. You must see it before you say no. I'm told the property is rundown but the price the owner has suggested is nothing short of a miracle."

But Yvette was even more reluctant than she dared admit. She feared to hurt the ladies' feelings. The countess was trying to help but sometimes she resembled a ram butting his head against a stable door. In Yvette's case, of course, the door would give way all too easily.

The countess was already waiting for Yvette when she appeared at the servants' entrance. She wore a stunning bonnet of embroidered velvet which Yvette knew was of her own design. It took only a short time for the carriage to reach St. John's Wood, an unfamiliar section of town to Yvette. She surveyed the walled houses with a sense of dismay until Lady Margaret clutched Yvette's sleeve.

"There. There it is," she said, stabbing her finger in the direction of a stone house set back from the street and sheltered by ancient oak trees. Tall, leaded windows were all but hidden by ivy with trunks as thick as a man's arm. Nine gabled windows and nearly as many fat chimneys punctuated the steeply slanted slate roof which covered the L-shaped house.

An iron gate leading to the entrance and the servants' door at the rear stood open, the only evidence that anyone had been there in years. Yvette loved it at first sight.

"But it's so charming...and so elegant."

The countess laughed. "And so impossibly dilapidated. My dear, I do believe I'm guilty of misjudgement. Perhaps we should leave after all."

"But it could be fixed up. All it needs is a little attention. Please. Can't we at least stop and look round?"

"As you wish. But remember, my girl, you can't afford to take on anything below acceptable standards. Appearances are everything."

Yvette hardly heard her as the carriage ground to a halt on the gravel driveway. She wanted this house as she had never wanted anything in her life.

The driver positioned the step and handed them down from the carriage, cautioning them against catching their gowns on the rose brambles that sprawled across the walkway.

Yvette raced up the wide steps to the main entrance which was guarded by a shallow stone archway and twin lanterns that were now solidly packed with encroaching ivy.

She noticed at once that the door was slightly ajar. "Someone's been here," she whispered to Lady Margaret as she picked her way through the vines.

"Indeed. That must be the owner. He promised to meet us here. Shall we inspect the interior, my dear, or have you already made up your mind to buy it sight unseen?"

Yvette giggled. "Am I so transparent? I feel as if I'm opening the lid of a treasure chest."

"Hardly that. At least not in the way you presume."

Yvette shot her a bewildered look, but the countess, her expression oddly inscrutable, motioned her inside.

A mustiness born of years of neglect assailed their senses. Lady Margaret quickly covered her nose with a lace handkerchief but Yvette was enchanted by the way the frail sunlight, filtering in through nearly obscured windows, illuminated the dust motes stirred to life by a sudden draught of air.

Her ladyship coughed. "It's so dark in here we'll never see a thing."

"The next floor should be brighter," Yvette said, moving from the wide entrance hall into what seemed to be a drawing room. "Let's explore the rest of the house. Perhaps the other windows are more open to the light." She studied the dark shapes of furniture that appeared not to have been moved in years. "The owner must have gone in through the servants' entrance. I see a pair of double doors slightly ajar on the far side of the room."

She found her way through a jumble of canvas-covered furniture, nearly falling over a large marble pedestal which must have once held a bust or a potted plant. And then a sound stopped her in midstride. The doors swung wide and there, silhouetted by a glare of light stood a tall man.

"Ladies, welcome to Waverly Lodge."

Even had it not been for the name, there was no mistaking that deep voice, that arrogant stance. Yvette was speechless but the countess apparently had herself better in hand.

"Ah, Lord Bancroft. There you are. I see you're prompt, as always."

"My apologies. I had intended to arrive earlier and open the windows to the light but I was delayed."

Yvette turned to the countess. "You knew he was going to be here? Surely you don't mean to tell me that *he* is the owner?"

"Indeed he is. Oh my, didn't I mention it?" she asked mildly. "It must have been an oversight."

"An oversight?" Yvette gave her a withering look but, unscathed, her ladyship moved out of the gloom into the sunlight of the adjoining room.

"I must say, Lord Bancroft, Mademoiselle Cordé and I are significantly disappointed in the condition of the house. We rather thought it would be more up to snuff." There was a breathlessness about her voice, that to Yvette, at least, signalled a calculated lack of interest.

Lord Bancroft smiled crookedly. "Is that so, countess? I could have sworn I overheard Mademoiselle Cordé speaking with a marked degree of enthusiasm just before I joined you."

The countess waved her lace handkerchief in dismissal. "Sounds do travel strangely in these old houses."

Yvette tried to restrain her excitement. "The house is larger than I imagined."

Lord Bancroft inclined his head. "You will soon fill it with people, mademoiselle."

"And most unkempt."

"It can easily be cleaned."

"And the grounds have grown into a jungle."

"The shrubs can be pruned and the gardens replanted."

"And there is far too much furniture."

"Some of which belongs to my mother. I reserve the right to remove select pieces of furniture from the house. The rest of it you may keep."

"I doubt that I can afford the house, at any rate."

"The price is far less than the value of the land, and I will permit you to make the payments in three instalments." His expression defied her to offer another rebuttal.

Yvette was ready to hand over her savings, but Lady Margaret touched her arm and spoke dubiously. "I fear, your lordship, that there is just too much work for mademoiselle to undertake on her own. Perhaps if you were to send some of your men over to clear the grounds . . . and if a half dozen or so of your domestics could assist in cleaning the house . . ."

He spoke with carefully guarded irritation. "And no doubt madam, you would like me to come along to supervise them?"

"What a splendid idea! I think, unless I am very much mistaken, that you have just struck a bargain, Lord Bancroft."

It was on the tip of his tongue to tell this harridan to send her so-called bargain to the devil, but at that moment he chanced to look over at Yvette and the rapt expression on her face was too much for him.

He walked over to stand beside her and it was as if the two of them were alone in the room. "Is this what you wish, mademoiselle? Do you wish to purchase my house?"

"I . . ." She looked quickly at the countess, who nodded vigorously behind his lordship's back. Yvette wet her lips with her tongue. "The . . . the answer is yes; that is, if the aforementioned terms are acceptable to you."

He nodded curtly and extended his hand. She hesitated for a fraction of a moment, then reached over to seal the bargain. The contact shook her composure but she managed to withdraw her hand despite his reluctance to let her go.

His voice was surprisingly husky. "Then it's done. I'll have my solicitor draw up the papers and you may take possession at once."

Lady Margaret flicked a bit of dust from her cape. "Then you may instruct him to send the papers on to *my* solicitor for approval."

Lord Bancroft's eyes narrowed with surprise. What had he got himself into? If he had expected this to be some trivial transaction that would put this inexperienced chit under an obligation to him, he had clearly deluded himself. His perception of Yvette was undergoing a change but, he told himself, he would be in control once she was out of the clutches of the countess.

It suddenly occurred to him that Yvette had made up her mind without having seen the rest of the house. But why shouldn't she? Even a female fresh from the farm must be aware that he had all but given her the house for pocket change.

By all that was holy she had better be worth it! He watched her walk towards a French window and push aside the dusty draperies for a better view of the garden. When he spoke, his voice was not as steady as he had hoped it would be.

"Now that you've taken the house, would you care to see the rest of it? Perhaps you'll wish to change your mind."

"Never!" she exclaimed, pressing her hands together. "It's perfect, or will be once I take it in hand. When may I expect your people to begin work on the grounds?"

"My people?" He looked thoroughly taken aback. "My good woman, surely you didn't take that exchange between the countess and me seriously, did you?"

"But naturally I did. What did you think I meant when I said the aforementioned terms prevailed?"

"I thought you referred to price."

"Well, of course, that was part of it. You can hardly expect me to clear the grounds and refurbish the house by myself."

"That's what servants are for. You, of all people, should know that, Mademoiselle Cordé."

When both women blanched Andrew knew he had gone a step too far. He silently cursed his abruptness, and the girl for the effect she had on him. He linked his hands together behind his back. "I beg your forgiveness, ladies. When I spoke of servants, I meant the domestics you are soon to require. Although I have only admiration for your courage and determination to better yourself, mademoiselle, my words sounded, even to my own ears, regrettably condescending."

They surveyed him with cool disdain. He felt beads of moisture begin to gather on his forehead but pride made him refuse to brush them away. He straightened. "Since the mistake was on my part, of course I will agree to your demands. The workmen shall be here in two days to begin clearing away the debris."

Lady Margaret beamed. "And of course my lord, you will be here to instruct them."

It was a statement rather than a question. Lord Bancroft knew when he was bested. He raised an eyebrow to Yvette. "And you, Mademoiselle Cordé, will be here to instruct *me* in what you wish to be done, I presume."

"I will try to get time off. However, I am still in Lord and Lady Berrington's employ."

"Nevertheless, I will not begin work without your supervision." He turned towards the countess. "And you also will honour us with your presence my lady?"

"Unfortunately, no, Lord Bancroft. My husband and I have much to accomplish in the next few weeks before we leave for the Indies."

"How unfortunate." Andrew failed miserably to suppress the grin that spread across his face. "But life is full of disappointments, countess. Somehow we shall have to survive without you." He strode towards another door that opened onto a wide corridor. "Mademoiselle, may I show you the rest of your house?"

"My house! I can hardly believe this is really happening," Yvette said as she all but danced through the carved oak doorway.

"Odd, isn't it?" Andrew spoke in a dry voice as he moved to join her. "I can hardly believe it myself."

Margaret Harrington followed behind them, her eyes bright, her grey curls bouncing with barely contained mirth and satisfaction.

They spent the rest of the afternoon going through the house room by room. The nine bedrooms, in addition to the servants' quarters, the reception rooms, the library, the second floor drawing room, the smaller, downstairs drawing room with its wide veranda, and, below stairs, the large, but decently arranged kitchen with its scullery and storage room below ground.

There was no time to visit the empty stables at the rear of the house or the greenhouse that Andrew said had once held prize roses, but he assured the ladies that these needed only a little work to bring them back to an acceptable state of repair.

They were discussing the condition of the marble fireplace in the library when the countess heard a noise in the adjoining room. "What was that, Lord Bancroft? Did you bring someone with you?"

"No. I came alone. The house was closed when I arrived." They listened, but there was only silence. "It couldn't have been our imagination. Stay here, ladies, and I'll see what it is."

Yvette picked up a candelabrum. "You can't go in there alone."

He motioned her to silence and slowly opened the door to the darkened room and stepped inside. "It's all right; we are quite alone. Just give me a moment to open the draperies."

Yvette and the countess followed in his wake. They heard the viscount moving about on the far side of the room. It took some time for Yvette's eyes to adjust to the semi-darkness. When they did, she heard a rustle, then felt something cross her foot and jerked back to see a tall figure next to her. She shrieked and began to beat upon his chest with all her strength.

"What th—" Andrew said, throwing open the draperies to the sun. "Really, mademoiselle." He looked down his nose at her. "You have no need to fly into hysterics. I think you'll find that the bear is already quite dead, and has been so for nearly fifty years."

"You might have warned me, sir. I am not used to living with dead animals."

He came over and took the candlestick from her trembling hands. Both she and the countess stared at the gaping hole in the bear's chest where sawdust and stuffing were sifting slowly onto the floor.

Yvette lifted her chin. "I hope it wasn't of great value."

Lord Bancroft shrugged. "The bear was nothing. Merely a memento of my grandfather's hunting trip to the Rhineland." He ran his fingers over the ornately carved silver candlestick.

"This, however is another matter. Luckily, in your childish outburst you selected a sturdy weapon, but I'm sure you would have chosen differently had you recognized its value. The candelabrum is one of a pair made nearly two hundred years ago by an Egyptian silver-smith."

He didn't notice the tight set of her mouth as Yvette reached for the weapon, or he would have thought twice before handing it back to her.

She smiled sweetly. "Thank you, my lord, for the lesson in antiquities. I'm sure I can find just the right place for the pair of them in my house."

"Regrettably, they are not included in the price."

"Ah, but you are wrong, sir. The agreement only extended to the removal of 'select pieces of furniture,' to use your words. Candelabra may indeed be considered furnishings, but they are not furniture. Am I not correct, your ladyship?" she asked, turning to the countess.

Margaret Harrington spread her hands. "What can I say, my dears? I am never one to become involved in domestic disagreements."

The viscount snorted, but was too put out to respond. Yvette went over to open another window to the light, then turned to view the room. "Oh, my, we can't have this. It's truly appalling."

"What? What do you mean?" Lord Bancroft demanded none too softly.

"Why this . . . this . . . graveyard of animal corpses," she said, sweeping her hand towards the walls that were crammed with trophies: antlers and zebra skins and pelts of unknown ancestry. "But then I'm sure these are valued family treasures which you wish to retain, my lord. In this case I will be pleased to make an exception to our agreement."

"You are too kind." He reached over to run his finger across the pointed spike of an antler. "And I know precisely what I'd like to use this for at this very moment," he said, levelling his gaze at Yvette.

She smiled winsomely. "I see we both share the same idea. Perhaps, instead, we should use it to kill mice. I've seen three since we arrived. And one ran across my foot."

"Fortunately for him, he didn't bite you. He would no doubt have been dead by nightfall."

The countess clasped her hands in delight. "You see, I knew the two of you would get on famously together. But enough for now, my dears. I promised Lady Emily we would be home by three."

CHAPTER THREE

THE NEWS that Yvette had purchased Waverly Lodge flashed through Berrington House in far less time than it had taken for her to make the original decision. There were mixed reactions. Lord and Lady Berrington were pleased and greatly impressed with the financial arrangements. If some of the servants exhibited envy, it was to be expected. Both Fredricks and Mrs. Grover seemed happy for her, but Fredricks marked the occasion by commenting drily that it would be impossible to find someone to replace her.

Lady Emily, who was resting in her bedchamber, held court with the countess and Yvette the next morning to discuss the many arrangements that must be made before Yvette left the protection of the Carstairs household.

"You will, of course, require a companion of some sort to forestall gossip," Lady Emily said.

"I hadn't thought of that."

"And of course a cook, a butler, a housekeeper and a gardener, to name a few."

"*Mon Dieu!* I cannot afford to pay so many servants."

The countess, looking enormously cheerful in a daffodil-yellow morning dress, sipped her chocolate, then put her cup down on the flower-sprigged saucer. "Nonsense, my girl. You can't afford not to. If you hope to establish yourself in Society you must learn to live appropriately. Trust me, it will be well worth your while." She toyed with the diamond rings on her fingers. "My husband is convinced that you are going to be the toast of London, and he is the best judge of people in all of London. Next to me, of course.''

Yvette started to laugh, but she saw that Lady Margaret was serious. Yvette's laughter dissolved into a cough, a ploy that did not go unnoticed by Lady Emily, who quickly stepped in to save the day.

''Our main concern here is to find a suitable companion. A woman of respectable birth who knows her way in the ton but has perhaps fallen on hard times.''

The countess clapped her hands. ''Udora Middlesworth!''

Lady Emily gasped. ''Truly, Margaret! Isn't Lady Udora something of an adventuress?''

''Oh, pooh. Just because Udora was widowed four times in ten years? Suffice it to say, Emily, gossip has it that all four men died with smiles on their faces. Udora may be close to thirty, but she is well-preserved, with a trim ankle and dimpled cheeks. Why, even the ladies seem to enjoy her company.''

''I'll grant that you know her better than I do, but would she be willing to take on such a charge?''

''I believe so. Money is of secondary importance to Udora. She was quite handsomely provided for by three of her four husbands, but she suffers easily from boredom.'' Lady Margaret paused for an instant, bobbing her head until her curls bounced. ''While I am the first to admit that Lady Udora is an upstart, she has always married for love, my dear, not for money. She has a good heart, and a likeable way about her. Besides, not the least of it is that she would settle for a paltry wage just to get back into the flow of London Society.''

''Then perhaps we should approach her.''

''My idea exactly. I'll see to it this afternoon.''

Lady Emily saw the bewildered look on Yvette's face. "Oh, dear. I suppose we should have consulted you first."

It was on the tip of Yvette's tongue to wonder why they should bother to do so at this late date, but she was so grateful for their help that all she could do was thank them. Besides, once she was on her own it was *she* who would be mistress of the house and make the decisions.

The papers from Lord Bancroft's solicitor arrived late that afternoon, a fact that surprised even the countess, who had prodded him into action. Mr. Harrington, who had arrived at Berrington House in time for tea, looked the papers over, then sent them by messenger to the home of his own solicitor for final approval.

Arrangements were then made to meet at Waverly Lodge the following day for the final signatures. Lord Bancroft had insisted on that location rather than his own residence. Yvette knew that it wasn't to save them the coach ride, as he had claimed, but to avoid a confrontation with Lady Bancroft. His mother was sure to be livid once she got wind of the transfer of deed.

Yvette slept only briefly that night and even then her dreams were haunted by a spectre in a black cape. Was she doing the right thing in letting her name become so well known? The knowledge of the chances she was taking nearly petrified her. One day she was bound to be discovered. But when... and by whom? She tried to push the thought from her mind, for it was too late to stem the tide of events she had already set in motion.

The next two days passed so quickly that they seemed less real to Yvette than her nightmares. Lady Emily was too encumbered by her pregnancy to offer much more than advice, but she sent along a retinue of servants to help with the house-cleaning. By the afternoon of the third day, close to exhaustion, Yvette wanted nothing more than to get settled in her new house and establish some kind of routine.

Lady Margaret gave her stamp of approval once they received word that Udora Middlesworth would arrive at Waverly Lodge before tea-time the same day. As a condition of her acceptance, Udora had insisted she bring her own equipage and driver and her own small staff of servants. Yvette was beginning to feel that she would at last make the move to her own establishment.

It was only on the day of her departure from Berrington House that her misgivings returned. She said her goodbyes to the other servants, who had become like a family to her. After that there was no question of hiring a dray to finish the chore of moving. The sum of her worldly possessions hardly filled two portmanteaux. At the moment of her departure, Lady Emily in her usual generous spirit, gave Yvette an iron-bound trunk filled with enough linens and quilts to establish a small household.

The greatest surprise came when Fredricks took Yvette's hands in his and wished her Godspeed. At the last minute he handed her a rectangular parcel. "A gift," he said, "in which to record the names of those fortunate ones privileged to visit you in your new home."

Yvette was touched. On a sudden impulse, she kissed his cheek and was rewarded by gasps from the assembled staff. Fredricks stiffened. "That's well and good, miss, but don't think I won't be calling round with my white gloves to see if you've kept the sills dusted," he quickly responded.

Everyone laughed. Yvette hugged the leather-bound book to her chest. "You can be sure, Mr. Fredricks, that I shall be honoured to include your name among my guests."

And then it was time for her to leave. Lord Berrington had instructed his driver to deliver her and her goods to the new house. She said her final goodbyes, feeling as if she were moving across a continent instead of merely to the other side of Town.

It was less than a half hour later when the carriage arrived at her home. Yvette felt an indescribable burst of pride. The gardeners had worked wonders at the front and sides of the house. The hedges were pruned, the walks trimmed, weeded and swept, the ivy tamed but not destroyed; just the way Yvette had instructed them. The lower limbs of the oaks had been cut back to allow sunlight to filter through, but the higher branches remained to form a green canopy over the parklike grounds. The tangle of gardens at the rear of the stone house would have to wait.

Inside the house, the dust had been obliterated from every surface on the main floor and two of the bedroom suites on the next floor. Windows had been opened to the sun while walls, floors and furniture had been scoured and rubbed to a soft patina with sandalwood oil and beeswax. The animal trophies had been relegated to a store-room until such time as Lord Bancroft could remove them, along with the few pieces of furniture he had selected to keep.

Having just finished adding fresh kindling to the fireplace, Yvette stood in the middle of the drawing room with her hands tucked into the sleeves of her gingham work dress. It occurred to her suddenly that she had seen Lady Emily in much the same stance the day her ladyship had become mistress of Berrington House.

And now Yvette was mistress of Waverly Lodge. If only her father and mother were alive to see how far she had come since that dreadful day in Paris. She was lost in her memories when a sound in the front entrance interrupted her thoughts. Another mouse? She wondered with less fear than curiosity, but it proved to be someone turning a key in the lock.

Lord Bancroft pushed the door open just as she entered the foyer.

"Ah, mademoiselle, there you are. I hoped to find you in. Are you here to stay?"

"Yes. This will be my first night in my new home." Her smile turned quickly to a frown. "But you shouldn't be here, Lord Bancroft. My chaperon has not yet arrived."

He stared at her, a slow smile spreading across his face. *Chaperon, indeed.* Surely she was jesting, but her eyes gave no hint of concealed laughter. She was becomingly bedraggled in her gingham work dress and sturdy apron. A few dark ringlets escaped from the sides of her mob cap and brushed her cheek, now ruddy from exertion. Or was she flushed by his unannounced presence? The thought warmed him and he decided to go along with her game of "great lady."

He swept a low bow and clicked his heels together. "I beg your forgiveness, my lady. I came only to see if you were provided with food and supplies. Without a carriage and servants to..."

"Oh, thank you, but I am quite well provided for. My housekeeper and servants are to arrive later today."

Lord Bancroft crossed his arms and tapped his fingers against the sleeves of his coat. *Servants? God's blood!* Had the girl already taken on a protector? It wouldn't surprise him one bit that some unprincipled rake might snap her up the minute she came on the market. But still, so little time had passed since she had decided to step out on her own. He muttered an oath then fixed her with his gaze.

"I seem to have underestimated you. May I ask, mademoiselle, if you are alone in the house?"

"I beg your pardon?"

He fumbled for the right words. By all that was holy, he would throw the rogue out of the house, once he learned his name. "What I mean to say is, have you someone to look after you?"

"Only as I said, my companion and chaperon, who will also arrive later today."

He saw the twinkle in her eyes and he clasped his hand behind his back. So! She was toying with him. She was damned clever, this one. Was she bamming him about having a chaperon? He was quite willing to go along with her charade, knowing that a goal too easily accomplished lost much of its thrill in victory.

He nearly broke into laughter but made an effort to look serious. "Surely there is a man in the house to protect you?"

"If I needed protection from anyone, sir, it would likely *be* a man, would it not? And by the way, how does it happen that you have a key to my house?"

He patted his vest pocket. "'Tis merely a precaution, mademoiselle, for your sake and mine. You will recall that the name Waverly still graces the gatepost. The house is not truly yours until the third payment has changed hands."

"Nevertheless, you have no right to..." She was interrupted by the rumble of the knocker on the front door.

She tucked a curl back into place. "That will be my chaperon, Lady Udora Middlesworth."

"Lady Middlesworth? Udora Middlesworth?" He repeated, dumbfounded. "That man-eater is going to be your chaperon?"

Yvette gave him a cool look. "Her credentials are quite acceptable. I'm told she was the daughter of a marquess. If you will excuse me?" she said, motioning him out of the way of the door.

He grasped her arm. "Yvette, surely you jest. The woman has buried three husbands in the last ten years."

"Four."

He looked appalled. "Four years?"

"No. Four husbands." Yvette looked pointedly at his hand on her arm. "And it appears, sir, that she is arriving none too soon. Will you kindly unhand me?"

He dropped his hands to his side. "This is a foolish decision, mademoiselle. It is enough that you have undertaken to better yourself, but taking on Udora Middlesworth is like aligning yourself with a . . . a . . ."

"Companion?" she asked.

"'Companion' was hardly the word I had in mind. There are less infamous courtesans in the flesh-house behind Covent Garden."

Yvette bristled. "Udora Middlesworth is certainly not a courtesan. She...she, er, simply likes having a man at her side. Under the blessing of the Church, I might add."

"A mere technicality."

The knocker sounded again, more loudly this time. Yvette moved towards the door and looked back over her shoulder. "Technicality? I do not know this word, but it matters not one whit to me what you think."

She opened the door to see standing in front of her a roundly endowed young woman dressed in bright green velvet with a plumed bonnet perched saucily atop a mass of carrot-red curls. The visitor smiled and dimples appeared in both her cheeks.

"Great pistachions! Margaret said you were a beauty, my love, but I had no idea you were so young. Oh dear, you do speak English, don't you? I should have asked Margaret, but everything transpired so quickly."

Yvette laughed. "Then you must be Lady Udora. I am Yvette Cordé. Won't you come in?"

Lady Udora giggled. "I'm afraid I have a bit of baggage. My driver has taken most of it round to the service entrance along with the rest of my entourage."

She looked over at Andrew and motioned towards the door. "I have another valise or two sitting at the end of the walk. Would you be a love and fetch them for me?"

Andrew stared down his nose at her. She wasn't at all what he had expected. Instead of a shameless hussy, Udora Middlesworth looked surprisingly young and appealing... for a woman who was getting close to thirty.

Yvette grinned. "Yes, my lord. Do be a dear and fetch her things to her bedchamber."

He unclasped his hands from behind his back and made a token bow. "As you wish, mademoiselle."

When he was safely outside, Yvette turned towards Udora. "You couldn't have known, Lady Udora. That was Lord Bancroft whom you just sent to retrieve your satchels. The house belonged to him before I bought it."

"Of course I know him when I see him. He is close to the top of the list. There's not a woman under the age of forty in all of England who wouldn't recognize his face."

"The list?"

"Why...of eligible men, of course." She walked into the corridor and peered into the drawing room. "Rather nice, isn't it? Too much furniture, though," she said, running her fingers across the keys of the pianoforte. "Some of it will have to go."

"Yes, I agree. Lord Bancroft plans to remove a few of the more important pieces as soon as he can arrange a place to store them."

Udora turned and planted her feet squarely in front of her, her hands on her hips. "Now then, let's have a look at you. Turn, turn!"

Yvette felt like an insect impaled upon the end of a pin. Udora nodded and her green plumes bobbed energetically. "Not bad, not at all bad. At least we have something to work with. A pity about your hair, though. It's very...um...black, isn't it? Oh well, a good hairdresser can work wonders. I trust you have a decent wardrobe."

"It's very limited, I fear."

"No matter. We shall change all that."

Lord Bancroft, on his second trip upstairs, kicked at the door that stood ajar. "What do you have inside this trunk, Lady Udora? A bed?"

Yvette gasped at his thinly veiled insult but Udora merely smiled. "No, my lord. My husbands have always managed to provide a bed, though on one occasion, little else. Harvey—he was my second husband, or was he the third? No matter. He kept a bed for every day of the week."

Andrew gave her a speaking look and she raised an eyebrow and added, "And if truth be told...sometimes they weren't enough."

His face grew red. Yvette closed the door a little too quickly. "If the trunk is too much for you, Lord Bancroft, just leave it at the foot of the stairs. My housekeeper and driver may be better able to carry it."

Andrew shifted the small trunk to his back and stomped up the stairs. "The gold suite, I presume."

"Yes. The third door on your left."

"I know where it is. I once lived here, you may recall."

Yvette looked quickly at Lady Udora who winked. "A bit of a handful, isn't he, love? Well, no matter. Men are more interesting that way. There's honey and there's spice. I've had them both in my forays into wedlock. Give me spice any day." She looped her shawl across the newel post, which was carved in the shape of a horn of plenty. "And by the way, I give you my word that I will not trespass in your domain."

"I beg your pardon?"

Udora waved a white-gloved hand towards the staircase. "His lordship, of course. It's obvious that he's smitten with you. Margaret told me as much and warned me off, so to speak."

"That's nonsense. Marriage is the furthest thing from my mind, not to mention the fact that he would hardly consider marriage to someone in my position."

"Marriage is, of course, the proper concern, but we must take things one step at a time. First we must open Society's doors to you. After that, who knows how far we may climb?"

She pulled her bonnet off and fluffed her mop of red curls. "Now then, where to start? It appears that we have our work cut out for us before we can begin entertaining."

"The fact of the matter is, I hadn't planned to entertain a great deal." Yvette gazed in dismay at her enthusiastic chaperon.

"But you must, of course. I consider it my duty to see that you take your proper place in Society. Entertaining is the first step."

Yvette was appalled. "I'm afraid I'm a bit past my prime to consider making a debut."

"Debut? Pistachions! I wasn't talking about a come-out. That's for girls who have to go looking for husbands. Your lack of introduction to Society is a minor obstacle which we shall overcome with connections and discreet, if not proper, behaviour."

Lady Udora punched the air with a bejewelled finger. "Mark my words, mademoiselle, it's the men who'll come looking for us, and not the other way round."

Yvette's laughter bubbled up. "Then I take it you have not removed yourself from the marriage market?"

"Whyever should I?" she said, showing her teeth and lifting her skirt to reveal a trim ankle. "Do I look toothless and hagged? I intend to find me a good, strong man, or two if need be, and establish my own permanent household before I grow old."

Yvette was saved from commenting by Lord Bancroft's re-entry. Above his carefully starched neckcloth his face was shiny with perspiration as he turned towards Yvette. "I have finished, mademoiselle, except for the wicker basket of kittens, which properly belongs in the stable."

Udora's hands flew to her breast. "The stable? Never! My boys have always had the run of the house."

"In *my* house, they do not," Andrew said with a grim set to his mouth.

"I beg pardon, my lord. I was under the impression the house now belongs to Mademoiselle Cordé."

"Not entirely."

Lady Udora snorted. "Then kindly tell me which portion is hers. The floor? The walls?"

Yvette gave Lord Bancroft a look that made him step backward. "My good sir, I'll not have you issuing orders to me or the members of my household. What I do here is no concern of yours."

"It is as long as my name remains on the gatepost."

"That can be easily remedied, by tomorrow at the latest."

"Enough! Enough!" he said, and stormed out of the house, leaving the front door standing ajar.

Udora had obviously enjoyed the confrontation. She was laughing as she followed him as far as the front entrance and retrieved the rather large willow basket filled with squalling kittens.

Her eyes twinkled as she brought them inside. "Good work, mademoiselle. You'll have him eating out of your hand in no time, if indeed he is not already doing so."

"It's more than likely he won't show his face round here again."

"Really, my dear girl, you are naive." She put the basket down on the floor and stood up. "Lady Margaret told me that you are partial to cats. That's fortunate, for otherwise I wouldn't have agreed to help you." She opened the lid and four young, very plump cats of assorted colours leapt free and spread out in all directions.

Yvette watched in amazement. "My goodness! They are well fed. They must be good mousers."

Udora snorted. "Never touch them. My boys like cream and an occasional bit of pilchard or herring at tea-time. Now then, show me my suite. I'm frantic to see the rest of the house."

THE NEXT EIGHT DAYS passed with amazing speed. Yvette sang at a small gathering at the home of Mr. and Mrs. Enrico Drazell, who owned a large importing concern. Making her first appearance in public since the death of her husband a year ago, Lady Udora was impressed by the surroundings, especially as they reflected her host's travels to China, Egypt and the Indies. She was, however, careful to point out privately to Yvette that opulence was no indication of social standing. Both women were made welcome not only as the evening's entertainment but as cherished guests.

When Udora remarked on this Yvette shrugged. "Don't expect the same treatment from the families of the haut ton. They tend to think of me as a servant." She laughed lightly. "Of course that is precisely what I am. They do however, pay me considerably more for my services as a singer than as a maid.''

"Pay you? My dear girl. Surely you don't accept a stipend?''

"Of course I do. How do you think I managed to buy this house?''

"Well, naturally I assumed it was a gift, albeit a conditional one, from the viscount.''

"Lord Bancroft? You assume too much, Lady Udora,'' Yvette said with measured indignation. "I am beholden to no man and that is the way I intend to stay.''

"Oh, dear. How dreary.'' Udora flounced across the library in her salmon-pink dressing gown. "Well, this does create another difficulty. You simply cannot continue to charge a fee for your performances. It is just too, too gauche, too *commercial*.'' She stood for a moment contemplating the flames in the fireplace. "Of course, if your hosts, and I emphasize the word, *hosts*,'' she said, slanting a look back over her shoulder at Yvette, "should insist upon presenting you with a gift of jewellery or furs, that would be quite another story.''

"But rather a risk, wouldn't you say? I assure you, Lady Udora, that I cannot afford to accept less payment than I am already receiving for my performances.''

"You handle these matters yourself?''

"No. Mr. Clarke, my pianist, makes the financial arrangements for me. Usually the payment is made to him and he subtracts his fee and passes the balance on to me.''

"Indeed. I think I might be well advised to have a talk with him. By the way, I spoke with Mrs. Eustace at the linen-drapers yesterday. She said she would send someone round tomorrow to look at our windows.''

"Tomorrow? But I am not ready to look for new draperies.''

"Of course you are. As I see it, you have no choice. Neither of us is getting any younger. We haven't a minute to lose in establishing an 'at home' day." She tapped her fingers against her cheek. "Thursdays, I think. How does that strike you?"

Knowing the matter was already settled, Yvette merely nodded her head helplessly.

If she expected difficulties in working with Udora's staff of servants, Yvette had a pleasant surprise. A married couple, Jarvis and Clara Campbell, had been with Udora for several years as housekeeper and butler at her country house in Hampshire. Clara was a compact little woman with neatly plaited grey hair and a quick smile that lighted her otherwise plain face. Jarvis, of medium stature and with snow-white hair, was remarkable only for his attentiveness to his wife, whom he obviously adored. The fact that they were a trifle long in the tooth did not significantly affect their enthusiasm. Yvette assigned them to the largest suite in the servants' wing.

Maggie McGee, a dark-haired Irish lass with shoe-button eyes and boundless energy, had been Udora's lady's maid through the last two marriages. She seemed delighted to take on Yvette's personal care for a reasonable increase in wages.

Yvette stood looking through freshly washed windows at the neatly pruned hedge which separated the formal garden from the stable. Everything was moving too quickly, but how could she complain? It had taken Udora a mere two days to uncover the fact that Mr. Clarke, her trusted pianist, was skimming money from payments which should have gone to Yvette. He had already been replaced by an equally talented and patient musician. Yvette had been less disappointed in Mr. Clarke than in herself. She had always thought herself to be a good judge of character and Udora's revelation had temporarily discomposed her. She decided to be more cautious in the future and also to be grateful that for the first time she need not face the world alone.

But now Yvette was becoming more popular as the days went by. She crossed her arms in front of her and smiled. Her dreams were beginning to take shape. Soon this house would be hers and hers alone. That, at least, she would have achieved.

OUTSIDE HER FRONT GATE, Andrew, Lord Bancroft, sat in his barouche smoking a cheroot. He scowled at the bitter taste and mashed the offending object in a tin. Why he had accepted the packet of cheroots from Greebers, he would never know. Greebers, of all people! The man was a backstabber, betting against him the way he had done. But he would get his comeuppance. The bet was already recorded on the books at White's, and each day the odds increased in his favour.

Andrew looked towards the house and a grin suddenly split his face. The sign, Waverly Lodge, remained snugly secured against the stone gatepost. It was just a question of time until everything fell into place.

He could picture it now. He'd take the air in Hyde Park, the proud owner of Greebers's new black-and-gold phaeton. And best of all, Mademoiselle Yvette Cordé would rest snugly under his protection. He'd have won his bet and he'd be the envy of every buck from London to Land's End. And only he would know how easy was his success.

CHAPTER FOUR

IT OCCURRED TO Andrew Waverly, Lord Bancroft, the following day when he arrived at the house unannounced, that perhaps he should have hedged his bet. He was met by Jarvis, the neb-nosed butler, who though small in stature, was nonetheless imposing. He bowed and stepped back, holding the silver tray at the ready to receive Andrew's card.

"Whom shall I say is calling, sir?"

"Lord Bancroft to see Mademoiselle Cordé."

"Is the mademoiselle expecting you, milord?"

Andrew frowned. "She will see me."

"I regret that mademoiselle is presently indisposed. If you care to leave your card, Lord Bancroft, she will see that you are informed when it is convenient for you to call." The look in his eyes accentuated the censure in his voice.

Andrew's temper blazed. "If you think I am going to beat the hoof out the door, you shall be disappointed, my good man. Now, kindly inform the lady I wish to see her."

Eyes narrowed, upper lip stiff as a frozen mackerel's, Jarvis inclined his head briefly. "If you will be so good as to wait in the salon I will see if she will receive you."

Andrew stood his ground until the butler climbed the stairs to the next floor. Only then did he make his way to the salon.

Some twenty-eight minutes and thirty-two seconds later, Yvette put in an appearance. It was Andrew's intention to set her properly down for keeping him treading the rug for so long, but one look at her freshly combed hair and her immaculate morning dress of forget-me-not blue, and the words stuck in his throat.

She dropped a curtsy. "Lord Bancroft. What a pleasant surprise. I wasn't expecting visitors so soon."

"Visitors, mademoiselle? Come, now. Surely I am not to be considered a mere visitor."

The slightly suggestive tone of his voice puzzled her until she remembered that he was still part owner of the house, that he still had furniture and personal effects to be removed.

She motioned him to a chair while she elected to sit at one end of a sofa. "Forgive me, Lord Bancroft. Of course I hope that we are to become friends as well as business associates."

"Friends?" He laughed. "What a charming way you have of putting it, mademoiselle. Is it your French heritage that lends such elegance to an, er, alliance?"

"Alliance? Do you refer to our business relationship?"

He laughed again. "I suppose one could call it that. However, I prefer to think less in terms of business than of pleasure." He moved over to the sofa where she was sitting. "To that end, Yvette, if I may be so bold, I have brought you a small gift."

"Oh but you must not," she said, moving aside to give him more space, unsettled by his tone and expression.

He moved an equal distance closer to her until their knees all but brushed. Yvette shot him a warning look but he distracted her with his honeyed tones. "It is nothing. Merely a token of my admiration for your lovely voice. I

insist that you take it, mademoiselle." He handed her a
small box tied with a gold velvet ribbon.

Yvette held it for a moment before attempting to untie
the extravagant bow, but the knot refused to give. Andrew was fast becoming impatient. His impatience turned
to frustration when he looked up to see Lady Udora
standing in the doorway. *Enter the dragon,* he thought
with considerable dismay.

"Ahem." She smiled and inclined her head in a greet-
ing to Lord Bancroft before turning her attention to
Yvette. "Perhaps, my dear, you would see better in the
chair nearest the window."

It was all too obvious what Lady Udora had in mind.
Yvette was reluctant to move. Sitting so close to Lord
Bancroft was stimulating in a surprisingly pleasant sort of
way. Besides, he was too much the gentleman to compromise her. But to save argument she moved to the other
chair and began to open the wrappings.

Lord Bancroft, who had risen when Lady Udora entered, remained standing, his hands clasped behind his
back. "My compliments to you, madam. You have worked
wonders with the salon. The woodwork hasn't sparkled so
in years."

"Thank you, my lord, although the credit must go to
our charming friend, who had overseen the completion of
most of the work before I arrived. There is too much clut-
ter, of course, but Yvette tells me that you will remove a
few select pieces of furniture."

"Indeed. As soon as I find a suitable place to store
them."

Yvette lifted the gift from the box to reveal a hand-
carved ivory lark perched on the side of a nest which held
three porcelain eggs. She gasped in pleasure. "How ex-

quisite! The bird looks so real that I expect it to fly away at any moment.''

Lord Bancroft looked as happy as if he had been given the gift. Both he and Lady Udora came over to stand beside her.

Lady Udora tilted her head. "How incredibly beautiful. I remember seeing another such carving among the treasures of Heatherwood Castle.''

Lord Bancroft smiled. "It was with considerable reluctance that the duke agreed to part with it.''

Yvette raised her face to look at him. "It is too much, Lord Bancroft. I really couldn't accept such an extravagant gift.''

Andrew's voice was husky. "Of course you can, and must, lest you offend both the duke and me. Is that not correct, Lady Udora?''

Udora's mouth turned up at the corners and her cheeks dimpled. "I see no breach of etiquette in Mademoiselle Cordé accepting the gift, my lord. I'm sure you are giving it with no expectations of obligation and no intention of extracting favours...of any kind. Is that not so?'' Her voice registered a subtle warning.

He hesitated only for the briefest moment. "I ask for nothing more than has already been implied.''

Yvette suspected a double-tongued message in his guarded words but his face showed no sign of deceit. As her fingers traced the inside of the carved nest she forgot about hidden meanings because she tripped a tiny lever and suddenly the bird lifted its head and burst into song.

"A music box!'' she exclaimed. "How enchanting.''

"A lark for a lark. Nothing could be more appropriate, mademoiselle. Say that you will accept my little gift.''

"How can I refuse? Thank you, Lord Bancroft. I shall be forever in your debt.''

He nodded. "Indeed."

Yvette looked at Lady Udora, who raised her eyebrows. Lord Bancroft continued. "It has come to my attention that you will be singing at Lord Crampton's soirée in a week's time."

"Yes, that is so."

"I would deem it a compliment if you would allow me to escort you, mademoiselle, and...er, of course the invitation includes Lady Udora," he said as he intercepted a look passed between the two women.

Lady Udora inclined her head. "How kind of you, Lord Bancroft. It would be our pleasure to accept. But a week seems so distant. We do hope that you will honour us with your company before that time."

Lord Bancroft had looked away but he swivelled his head towards her. *God's blood! Was the woman flirting with him?* Widowed she might be, and four times over, but there was still something of the coquette about her. He ran his finger around his neckcloth.

"It was not my intention to make a constant pest of myself, Lady Udora, but it would please me to be considered a welcome guest."

She smiled, showing a row of rather pointed, very white teeth. "It isn't official as yet, my lord, but I think Thursdays are to be our at-home night." She shivered and crossed her arms in front of her.

Lord Bancroft brightened. "You look chilled, my lady. Would you not be more comfortable with a shawl?"

Yvette spoke. "May I fetch one for you, Lady Udora? It's rather cool away from the fireplace." She started to rise but Lord Bancroft put his hand on her shoulder.

Lady Udora dimpled. "Nonsense. I'm perfectly capable of running my own errands. I refuse to be treated like an aging aunt when I am only a few years beyond my come-out. If you'll excuse me, I'll be but a moment," she said, moving gracefully towards the doorway.

Once she was out of sight, Lord Bancroft took a seat across from Yvette. This time there was no doubt that his knee grazed hers. He reached over and cupped his fingers beneath her hands where they still held the lark's nest.

"Alone at last, *ma petite*. I began to despair of ever seeing you without someone hovering over us."

Yvette started. When she spoke there was a breathless quality to her voice which was due to the unaccustomed contact of his hand against hers. "Caution, sir. Your gift is exquisite and I shall treasure it always, but we must not be tempted towards undue familiarity." She laughed lightly, hoping to soften the censure in her words.

Unfortunately, Lord Bancroft mistook her laughter for a subtle form of sarcasm. "Familiarity, indeed!" He lifted her hand to his lips. "I predict that we shall become *very* familiar in the days to come, my lady lark."

Yvette's face turned a rosy pink and she jumped up. "I don't know what you mean, monsieur."

"I think you do, my dear."

"If you mean that we shall become good friends, then I look forward to it with pleasure. If, on the other hand you intend us to become—"

She was interrupted when Lady Udora swept into the room, a brilliant yellow shawl swirling about her shoulders. "Here I am, at last. You were right, Lord Bancroft. A shawl is a decided comfort."

He stood, frowning. "You must have run all the way, Lady Udora."

"Indeed? I thought it took me a rather long time. Well, never mind. Now then, what were we discussing?" she said, ensconcing herself on a ladder-back chair. "I believe it was our at-home nights." She motioned to the sofa. "Do sit down, both of you. I'll ring for refreshments."

Yvette bent down to place the lark's nest on an ornately carved table. "That won't be necessary, Lady Udora. Our guest was about to leave." She surveyed him with a cool gaze. "Is that not correct, Lord Bancroft?"

"Now that you mention it . . ." He saw the challenge in her eyes and he slapped his thigh. "No, by gad. I think I'll stay a while longer. With your permission, of course, Lady Udora."

She beamed. "But of course, do sit down. Or would you be more comfortable in the library?"

He raked Yvette with his gaze. "Yes, there is a noticeable chill in this room."

Yvette lifted her chin. "I doubt, sir, that you will find the library any warmer."

His mouth hardened for a moment and then a slow smile spread across his face. "Don't tell me the fire has gone out."

She smiled. "I wasn't aware that the tinder had been lit, my lord."

"Come now, mademoiselle. Surely you remember that the fire was kindled the moment you bought the house. Not once have we allowed the embers to die out."

Yvette made a determined effort to stifle her laughter. "We? You must be mistaken, sir. I have not so much as added a single twig to the fire." She picked up the golden velvet ribbon and pleated it between her fingers. "Perhaps you've had someone else fanning the flames."

"There is no one else, I assure you."

"I find that hard to believe. It is a well-known fact that you have an endless number of . . . of those waiting to, ah, tend your hearth."

His mouth twitched. "Never confuse gossip with fact, Mademoiselle Cordé."

Looking discomfitted, Udora tossed the end of her shawl over one shoulder. She felt the conversation was getting a little too intimate, even for her sophisticated taste, and decided to intervene. "I appear to have missed something. If you are concerned about the temperature, I can vouch for the fact that there has been a warm fire burning all morning."

Andrew beamed his approval. "You see, I was right. Shall we remove ourselves to the library?" His gaze challenged Yvette to defy him, a challenge she could hardly refuse.

"An excellent idea," she said, clasping her hands together. "I'm sure the two of you will excuse me. It is nearly time for Mr. Armbruster, my new accompanist, to arrive to begin practise for my next concert."

Lord Bancroft stopped dead in his tracks. "Forgive me. I had no idea I was interrupting your schedule. In that case I shall take my leave."

Lady Udora took his arm in a remarkably strong grasp. "Nonsense, my dear Lord Bancroft. You've only just arrived. Come. I've asked Jarvis to serve brandy in front of the library fire."

"Thank you, Lady Udora, but . . ."

"No excuses, now. Besides, I want you to see what we've done to the mantelpiece."

In spite of himself, Lord Bancroft cast a pleading look back at Yvette as he was being towed down the corridor. She smiled and waved.

"I look forward to seeing you next week at the Crampton soirée. Lady Udora and I shall be ready at seven."

He stopped and turned at the door to the library. "I trust mademoiselle, that you will stay warm and that the climate will have improved by then."

Yvette's laughter trilled down the corridor. "One must learn to live with the weather, my lord, for there is little one can do to change it."

Andrew muttered an oath. Had it not been for the stranglehold Lady Udora had on his arm he would have had the last word, but Yvette had disappeared before he could think of one.

IN THE DAYS that followed, Yvette found it hard to concentrate on her music. It was important that she practice her singing every day. Of course Mr. Armbruster could not be expected to accompany her at her daily rehearsals since he was otherwise employed at the Fenstercroft house as a gentleman's gentleman, but Lady Udora was a willing if unskilled accompanist. That she complained constantly about the quality of the sound from the ancient pianoforte did not signify, since there was no other instrument available.

"Yvette, my dear," Lady Udora said when they had finally settled on a programme for the Crampton soirée, "your voice is incomparable. No wonder you are in such demand. Did I tell you I turned down two engagements yesterday?"

Yvette looked up sharply. "Really, Lady Udora, I wish you hadn't done so. You must know how I depend on these appearances to pay for this house. I still have insufficient funds to meet the second payment, not to mention the one to follow soon after that."

"Appearances, my dear, is what I'm concerned about. The Drazelles and the Mockerbys could hardly afford to give you a suitable gift in recognition of your having favoured them with your time. If we let them fob us off with some cheap gewgaw, the afterclap would be such that your income would eventually decline. As it stands, the Cramptons are sure to try to outdo the Gallsworthys and the Tarkingtons will try to make the Cramptons look clutch fisted, to say the least.''

"I suppose you're right." Yvette walked over to the window and her gaze was drawn to a shuttered carriage standing near the entrance gate. A pair of greys moved restlessly as if they had been held too long in one position. Her stomach tightened. She called Lady Udora to the window.

"Do you recognize that carriage? This is the third time I've seen it standing there."

"I've no idea who it might be but I'm sure they mean us no harm. The carriage is well kept and the horses certainly look prime. It's probably just some admirer."

"But no one, save the Berringtons and Lord Bancroft, knows yet that I've purchased the house. It could hardly be an admirer."

Lady Udora looked pained. "I was thinking of my own following, Yvette, my dear. Not yours."

"I'm sorry. It never occurred to me." She hastened to add, "Only because it has been hardly a year since you lost your last husband."

Udora gave her a dry look. "It was Reginald who expired, not I. He would have not wanted me to mourn overlong." She tapped her lower lip. "I wonder...should we send a servant to enquire? Perhaps it is someone important. He could prove to be interesting, you know."

"No! I'm sure whoever it is will leave in a little while and as you say, he apparently means us no harm."

"Curious, though, isn't it?"

Yvette turned away from the window. "Curious" was hardly the word. "Frightening" might be more appropriate, but she could hardly confide the reason for her distress to Udora Middlesworth. There was, in fact, no one in whom she could confide her fear of being discovered. She must just carry on as usual.

It was less than an hour later when Lord Bancroft arrived, unannounced as always. Yvette had entertained him on two occasions but had put him off twice during the week by giving strict instructions to Jarvis to say that she was out.

This time Andrew was not to be fobbed off. Unfortunately, Lady Udora was in her bath and it would be some time before she could be decent. Rather than cause Jarvis undue harassment, Yvette seized a shawl and made her way downstairs.

"It's all right, Jarvis. You may show Lord Bancroft to the library."

Lord Bancroft's gaze flew to the stairway. "So, you are at home after all, mademoiselle. And a good thing, too, I might add."

"Indeed? Is there some urgent business you wish to discuss with me?" She kept her voice cool and businesslike.

"Call it what you may, but be warned, I do not take well to being bamboozled." Bancroft's own voice was barely civil.

Jarvis helped him off with his cloak and looked down his nose at Lord Bancroft. Not an easy trick, considering that his lordship topped him by a good head and shoulders. "This way to the library, my lord." His tone was glacial.

"I know the way, confound it. This is my house."

Yvette was puzzled by his outrage. She stopped long enough to tell the maid to prepare a tray of apricot brandy and cakes to be brought to the library. Perhaps the wine would serve to mellow him, though why should she pander to his moods?

He was standing facing the fire with his back to her when she entered and closed the door. He cut a fine figure in his buff nankeens and rust-coloured waistcoat. His Hessians were polished to a high sheen; his hair was walnut-brown and thick where it curled round the thong at the back of his neck. Lady Udora was right. This was a man few women could ignore.

"Lord Bancroft," Yvette said as she came into the room.

He turned. "I didn't hear you come in."

"You can be sure that everyone from here to Cavendish Square heard *your* impromptu arrival," she told him coldly. Courtesy, if not good breeding, should have alleviated that scowl before he appeared in public.

"As they may well have two days past, when I was so unceremoniously turned away when I came to call. This farce shall end today." He bit off the words.

"Farce? I do not know what you mean, sir." Yvette's chin lifted and her level gaze did not waver.

His face felt warm, and it had nothing to do with the heat from the fire. God's blood, this woman could act. She had missed her calling when she took up singing. He resisted an impulse to seize her and shake her until the combs fell from that mop of black curls. She stood like a queen, calm, controlled, and indescribably desirable in the simple gown and shawl which she wore like a ceremonial robe.

Her eyes flickered with a challenge. "And before we go on, Lord Bancroft, I must tell you I resent the fact that you continue to claim ownership to my house."

"Your house! *Your* house? It is hardly *your* house."

"What do you mean? It will be, when I have completed the two payments which remain. Need I remind you that they are not yet due? Remember also that I have your signed agreement."

His eyes glittered dangerously. "An agreement that covered only the fundamentals, of course, since I am too much a gentleman to force you to put to paper the more intimate details of our alliance."

She laughed even as she shook her head. "What nonsense is this? I agreed to nothing which was not included in the contract. Surely you are jesting."

His face went from red to white. "Don't think me a fool, mademoiselle. Nor do I consider you a pea-brained goose. It was out of respect for your sensibilities and your obvious intelligence that I chose *not* to spell out the details of our agreement."

"Then I suggest you spell them out now." All laughter had vanished from her face.

He swore softly, then turned and strode to the window. Things were not going well, not going well at all. He stood there for a few tense moments, then turned to face her. Despite the fire in her eyes and the firm set of her chin, she looked infinitely appealing, a fact that made his task more difficult than he cared to admit. What was going on? She wasn't the first petticoat he had taken under his wing. Never once had he had the least difficulty in stating what was expected of the girl and what she could expect from him. *Expect from him . . .*

"God's blood!" He smacked his forehead. "So that's it!" he said reaching for his money bag. "Did you think it ungenerous of me not to have given you your allowance at the start? Forgive me, my pet." He tossed a bag of coins onto the table and waited expectantly. She stood as if frozen to the spot. He smiled. "Go ahead. Take it. If you please me, there will be a similar sum in a week's time."

Had Yvette not been so furious she would have giggled at the schoolboy expression on his face. But this was no laughing matter. How dare he even imagine that she might consent to be his mistress? For that, beyond doubt, was what he was suggesting.

She bent down and picked up the bag of coins. "So this is what you think of me," she said, jingling the coins. "A paltry sum, don't you agree?" She kept the anger from her voice.

He gave her a look of triumph. "Of course! You misunderstand, mademoiselle. These are gold, nothing less. I would not be so miserly as to insult you."

"The evidence proves otherwise, sir. Your inference is in itself an insult." Her control snapped. "How dare you, sir? How dare you presume to imagine I might become your—or anyone's, mistress!"

"It needed no imagination." Lord Bancroft was just as angry. "Why else should I sell my house to you for a pittance? Pocket change, no more. Do you think I simply throw money away without any thought of return?"

"You are no stranger to the gaming tables at White's, I collect," she retorted swiftly.

His face flushed, as if he was suddenly embarrassed, but he recovered quickly. "If and when I gamble, the stakes are high and I make it a point never to lose. This was not a wager we entered into, Mademoiselle Cordé, but a bona fide business arrangement."

"Agreed. That is the way I interpreted it." She spoke more calmly. "I assumed that you were willing to sell the house for a paltry sum simply because you no longer wished to assume the burden of maintaining it."

"The house is worth a hundred times what you paid for it."

"Then I shall be forever in your debt," she said, flushing at the implications of her words. "What I mean to say is that I am grateful to you for your generosity. But the truth is, I shall never become your mistress. The thought has never entered my mind."

He was too angry to speak, but something in her voice made him look twice. Her eyes gave her away. She was lying. It was probably true that she had no intention of coming under his protection, but not for one minute did he believe that the thought had not entered her mind.

A smile curved the corners of his mouth. She had nearly hit on it when she mentioned the gambling in which he occasionally indulged at White's. Fortunately she was unaware that the latest high-stakes wager to be entered in the books involved her—and him.

His smile caught Yvette unawares. He was so sure of his own charm that he still was not convinced she was unavailable to him. The further evidence of his conceit galled her.

She forced a smile of her own. "Under the circumstances I will forgive you for your misunderstanding of my character, providing you never bring up the subject again. And now I suggest that you take your departure."

She jingled the bag of coins again and weighed them in the palm of her hand. "But another point, my lord, since you will never discover it for yourself. Do not presume to judge me by your previous misadventures. I am worth far more than this." She tossed the bag of coins to him and it fell at his feet.

He bent slowly to pick it up. Then, in a startling gesture, he seized her by the shoulders and kissed her soundly on the mouth.

CHAPTER FIVE

"HOW DARE YOU!" Yvette lashed out at him. She would have struck him, but he grasped her wrists and held them immobile. Their gaze met in a fierce duel in which neither would admit defeat. "Andrew Waverly, you are entirely without principle. I refuse to be treated like some . . . some poor light-skirt who hasn't a penny to pinch."

"I would never reduce you to that level, mademoiselle. It was my intention to offer you a generous sum as well as my not insignificant protection. If you will but think, I have already given you a house, the deed to which is penned in no name but your own."

"You have *given* me a house? This house was no gift, my lord. It came to me as the result of a very careful business transaction. And I demand that you let go of my hands."

His eyes finally released hers, but before she could protest he brought her hands to his lips and kissed her palms, each one in turn. The touch of his mouth against her skin was so unnerving that Yvette felt herself go weak at the knees. Before she could change her mind, she summoned all her strength and pulled away from him.

"You are utterly mad, sir. If my chaperon were here you would never have attempted such an indiscretion. Kindly leave before I am forced to summon my butler."

"I do not intend to leave until you admit you have tried to bamboozle me. You knew full well what the unwritten terms were when I agreed to put the house in your name."

"I knew nothing of the sort. Now leave at once." She pointed to the door.

"Never!" he repeated stubbornly.

Yvette ran to the fireplace and grasped a poker. Turning it end for end she brandished it in front of her like some lethal weapon. "If you do not leave at once I refuse to be responsible for my actions," she said, preparing to strike him over the head.

Instead of taking it from her, as she knew he easily could, he began laughing. "All right. You win this round, mademoiselle. I will go, but I promise you, this contest is not over."

"There will be a snowstorm in July before I consent to be *your* doxy, my lord."

He started towards the door with Yvette following close behind, poker at the ready. At the last minute he turned and pointed a finger directly at her nose. "Be advised, Mademoiselle Cordé, that I shall be here at seven tomorrow night to take you to the Crampton soirée."

The poker struck the door as he hastily closed it behind him. Yvette turned to see Jarvis enter the room.

"Stoking the door frame, miss?" he asked.

"No, I..." And then she saw the glint of mischief in his eye and she lowered the poker. "No, Jarvis, just tidying up."

"Yes, miss. Do you wish me to send his lordship packing next time he comes calling?"

Yvette wrapped her fingers round the poker and looked through the long narrow window to the entrance gate where the curricle was spraying gravel in a hasty departure. "No, Jarvis. That won't be necessary. I doubt that

Lord Bancroft will create any further disturbance. He is entirely harmless."

"Very good, miss." He bowed and returned to his work in the salon.

Harmless? Harmless, indeed! Yvette mused on her way upstairs. Her palms still felt the pressure of his mouth. True, it had been a comparatively innocent kiss, but still a kiss to be reckoned with, for she was far more unsettled than she wished to admit. Andrew Waverly, Lord Bancroft, was too charming, too exciting and far too sure of himself. Small wonder the man had half the women of the haut ton fawning over him. She threw her shawl over her shoulder in a determined gesture. Fortunately for her, this house was in her name. She was safe, at least for the moment.

Lady Udora was dressed to attend the shops when Yvette arrived at her door. "Was there someone come to call?" she asked, coming into Yvette's sitting room.

"It was only Andrew Waverly."

"Only? Really, my dear. Frequent as they are, a visit from Lord Bancroft could hardly be considered insignificant."

"I fear I must agree with you. He was under the impression that he had *carte blanche* to call whenever he chose. He even went so far as to presume that he is to become my protector." Yvette tossed her black curls indignantly.

"Gracious!" Lady Udora blinked at her. "We can't have that. I shall speak to him."

"No, please, Lady Udora. I pray don't do that. I have set him down quite properly. I doubt that he will approach me again."

"I wonder," Udora said thoughtfully. She looked at Yvette. "I assume, then, that we must procure another escort to the Crampton soirée tomorrow evening?"

"No. Lord Bancroft will be here at seven."

"In truth?" Udora said with a quizzical expression on her face. "If that is so, I fancy he is not as fully dissuaded as you might think. Be careful, Yvette. The man is clever. He has a reputation for getting what he wants."

They looked up as Jarvis entered the room to announce that the carriage was waiting to take them to Bond Street.

The shops were crowded that afternoon and the selections were far too extravagant for Yvette's taste. The gowns she found were too ornate, or too flimsy, or the wrong colour. After a while, they stopped for tea and then, catching their second wind, had their driver take them to Harrington's, the shop that had once belonged to Cyrus Grimstead before Lord Berrington had him arrested. Lady Margaret and Mr. Harrington had taken over the store, which had become well known for its exquisite, if outrageously expensive, gowns.

A few gowns were finished and on display as they entered the store. Yvette was immediately drawn to a russet velvet dress which had a scalloped hem that revealed an underskirt of brown satin. The russet yoke was cut low, with scallops piped in satin to match the skirt. Small roses made of the same rich, brown satin adorned the left shoulder.

"What do you think, Lady Udora?" Yvette asked. "Is it too daring?"

Udora dimpled. "It would hardly do if one had to bend to tie a shoe, but I fancy you'll manage quite well. take it. It will be perfect with your amber pendant."

But when Yvette asked the price, she discovered it was far too costly to fit her small budget.

"Pistachions!" Lady Udora proclaimed. "You must wear the best. Have them put it on your bill."

"I'm afraid I can't afford to keep an account. I pay for goods as received."

"Appalling. No lady of quality pays on receipt. It's too, too gauche."

"But it's the only way I can manage to keep up with my debts. No. I've made up my mind. I'll wear the grey brocade for this concert."

Udora threw up her hands. "Fie! You will be the death of me yet. Very well. Take it off and be done with it. As for me, I think I'll treat myself to this little fur capelet. And while they're wrapping it, we can go across the street to the chocolate shop. I see some of my friends stopping there."

Yvette was ready in a surprisingly short time. They found the chocolate shop crowded with weary shoppers and it came as a surprise to Yvette that Udora was greeted at every hand.

When seats became available, they were immediately joined by several other young women. Udora made the introductions. "This is my sister-in-law, Candide Hamilton, my sister-in-law and brother-in-law, Charlotte Kinkaid and Sir Peter Kinkaid, my nephew-by-marriage, Horace Jepson, and my good friend Oscar Davidell."

Yvette exchanged greetings. "My goodness, I had no idea yours was such a large family, Lady Udora."

They all laughed and Candide Hamilton spoke, her enormous brown eyes twinkling. "I daresay, if Udora collected every one of the relatives from her various marriages, there wouldn't be room in Covent Garden to hold them all."

Udora nodded. "So true, my dear. And I wouldn't forsake a single one of them. My dear husbands—all four of them, I might add—had the good taste to come from excellent stock. If I can do as well in my next marriage I'll count myself blessed."

They all leaned forward and seemed to hold their breath. Oscar Davidell ran his tongue over his mustache. "Aha! So you already have some young man in mind. May I ask who the next victim is to be, Udora, my love?"

She arched her eyebrows. "Victim? Really, Oscar. What fiddle-faddle. You know very well that my husbands died happier for having known me. But as to your question: sadly, I must confess I've had little time to select the lucky man. I've been utterly out of circulation for nearly a year now, but thanks to Mademoiselle Cordé, I plan to get back into the Season."

A cheer went up round the table. Those fortunate enough to sit close by enough to hear the conversation nodded their approval. A party was not a party until Udora Middlesworth arrived with her lively spirit, her dimples, and her neatly turned ankle. She had worn black gloves for too long.

Udora smiled in acknowledgement. "Thank you, thank you indeed. And as we speak, I am reminded to invite each one of you to a little gathering on Thursday evening. Mademoiselle and I will be receiving on a regular basis, now that we are settled in. We do so look forward to seeing each one of you. Is that not so, Yvette?"

Yvette could do little more than stammer, but all seemed to take it as an affirmative reply, for when they took their departure ten minutes later, they promised to be in attendance. As Udora and Yvette stood to leave, a portly woman in purple satin accosted them.

She touched a folded pink parasol to Udora's arm. "Lady Udora, I thought I recognised your voice. It is so good to know that you have re-entered the flow this Season."

Udora lifted her chin. "Lady Florence. How nice to see you. May I present my friend, Mademoiselle Yvette Cordé."

Lady Florence beamed. "Though it is true we have not met, I have heard so much about you, mademoiselle. It is my most fervent wish that you will consent to sing at one of my soirées."

Udora gave Yvette no chance to respond. "Ah, Lady Florence. You do us no small honour, but I regret to say, mademoiselle has such a generous following that it seems unlikely there will be an opportunity to grant your kind request. Of course we will do our best."

Lady Florence flushed to the roots of her hennaed hair. "I assure you, Udora, we can pay whatever you charge."

Udora looked appalled. "Please do not think of it, my lady. Mademoiselle would never stoop so low as to charge a fee." She touched a hand to her cheek in a demure gesture and batted her eyelashes. "Of course if one is offered a gift of jewellery or a bit of fine porcelain...one could hardly refuse."

The woman moved closer. "I am quite prepared to be generous."

"Of course you are, Lady Florence. I didn't doubt that for one moment." She patted the older woman's arm. "Perhaps if you could send me a letter giving all the details..."

"Yes, yes. At once."

"And if you would care to join us on Thursday, we would be so pleased. Is that not so, Yvette?"

"I...er...yes, of course."

Udora nodded her approval. "And now we must go. So much to do, you know. Yvette is in concert at the Crampton's tomorrow. Of course you'll be there."

"No, unfortunately we have a previous engagement."

"Regrettable. Until Thursday, then," Udora said, leading Yvette towards the door. When they were out of earshot Udora chuckled. "Previous engagement, pistachions! I'll warrant she wasn't invited. Come now. We've a mountain of work to do before tomorrow."

They made two more stops before Udora had finished her errands. During these, she managed to invite another dozen couples to their Thursday night salon. When they finally arrived home they had to wait for a dray to clear the lane before they could pass through the entrance gate.

"Whatever are they doing here?" Udora wondered aloud. "Did you order something to be delivered?"

"No," Yvette responded. "I rather suspect that Lord Bancroft has finally found space to store the few pieces of furniture he wished to retain."

"Splendid. And just in time for our salon on Thursday. I have been puzzling over what to do with the crush of furnishings in the drawing room. Such heavy pieces only overwhelm a party and stifle conversation."

The carriage deposited them at the front door and the butler rushed out to assist the women with the numerous parcels they had purchased at the shops. Jarvis looked uncommonly distraught. He glanced furtively from the house to Yvette, then back again.

"What is it, Jarvis?" she asked. "Is something amiss?"

"Yes, mademoiselle. I didn't wish to be the one to tell you."

"Tell me what? I saw the dray. Did Lord Bancroft come for his furniture?"

Jarvis visibly relaxed. "You knew, then?" He smiled. "I feared that his lordship might have been stealing a march on your property."

Yvette laughed as she and Lady Udora preceded Jarvis into the foyer. "Lord Bancroft has his faults, but I'm sure he would never stoop to cheat us. He is after all, a gentleman of considerable standing.''

Udora, who had walked ahead of her, let out a piercing shriek. "Gentleman, you say? The man is a glimflashy, a . . . a bawbling demi-devil . . . a . . ."

Yvette rushed to her side. "Really, Lady Udora. How can you . . ." Yvette stopped dead in the hall, then dashed to look quickly into several rooms. Hardly a single stick of furniture remained. She put her hand to her mouth. *"Pas possible!"* Her voice echoed hollowly in the room. "He's taken every last stick!"

Jarvis stood back a safe distance behind the two women, whom he perceived correctly to be in an exceedingly volatile state. "And there's more, miss. The morning room and the drawing room."

Yvette clenched her hands into fists as she endeavoured to keep her voice calm. "Did he leave anything behind?"

"There are a few rooms he didn't get to, miss; the kitchens, of course, the library, the dining room, the servants' quarters, and the bedrooms."

Udora lifted her eyebrows. "The bedrooms?" She spoke *sotto voce*. "I wonder, my dear, if he's trying to tell you something?"

Yvette blanched. *"Il me le payera cher!"*

Jarvis apparently read the murderous look in her eyes and made a discreet departure to the kitchen. Udora put her arm across Yvette's shoulders. "That's right, sweetling, we'll make him pay for this, but never mind for now. We can manage. I've been dying to refurbish this mausoleum . . . put some life into it. We're both too young to be buried in a musty tomb."

"But I can't afford to buy furniture. It's all I can do to pay for the upkeep."

"What's mine is yours, when it comes to maintaining our position, or—" she lifted an eyebrow "—or in this case, bettering it. I can quite well afford to buy whatever we need to keep up appearances."

"It's so kind of you, but I can't let you do that." Yvette spoke firmly. "You may need your money one day."

"Nonsense. I have buckets of it to spare. Besides, it is my intention to marry again before I become too long in the tooth to turn a man's head. And I intend to marry up this time." She dimpled. "Although I must admit, if the right young man came along I would probably be too weak to refuse him."

Yvette smiled in spite of herself. "I know you are simply trying to cheer me, Lady Udora."

Udora looked surprised. "Nothing of the sort. I merely spoke the truth. Now then, let's decide our next move. Whatever you do, Yvette, don't let Lord Bancroft know he's got the better of you."

"I intend to set him down quite properly."

"And let him know that he's won this match? Don't be a ninnyhammer. When he comes to escort us to the Crampton soirée, you must greet him as if nothing's amiss."

Yvette gave her a dry look. "And where would you suggest we have him sit while he's waiting for us?"

"In the parlour, of course. Where else?"

Yvette regarded her with a puzzled expression; then a smile lighted her face. "Of course, an excellent idea, I assure you. Furthermore, I'm sure it will take an inexcusably long time for me to dress."

Udora smiled. "Indeed, and the fire in the grate will most surely go out long before we are ready."

"Don't you think that ha'past six tomorrow night might be the perfect time for the maids to wax the parlour floor? A double coat might be just the thing."

"But it won't be dry by the time . . . Oh, yes. I see."

"Good. Then I'll give the orders."

It wasn't until the middle of the night that Yvette remembered that the pianoforte was also gone. Ancient as it was, it was the only means she had of rehearsing her music. And then she remembered the guests Udora had invited for a Thursday night salon. Well, there was nothing for it but to inform them all that it had been cancelled. If only she knew who they all were. Udora had offered a blanket invitation to anyone within the sound of her voice. Knowing the current trend for Society nabobs to hop from party to party and to arrive with a friend or friends in tow, half of London could show up on her doorstep come Thursday evening. That would be nothing short of social disaster.

She groaned. It took an effort, but Yvette managed to banish it from her mind. First, the concert; after that she would deal with whatever misfortune Fate conspired to hand her. She had survived almost insurmountable odds once before. She could do it again.

As it happened, Fate, in the guise of Lady Udora, took a hand in dressing Yvette for the Crampton soirée. When Yvette asked Maggie to fetch her grey gown from the armoire, she instead brought out the russet velvet and satin gown Yvette had admired so much the previous day.

"What is this? Where did this come from?"

Maggie McGee smiled mischievously. "'Tis from 'er leddyship, miss. She asked me to 'ide it in your cupboard until 'twas time for you to dress for the concert."

"But I can't accept such an expensive gift."

"Neither can you 'urt 'er feelings, miss. I knows 'er leddyship, miss. She'll not be pleased above 'alf if you refuse to wear it."

"It is beautiful, isn't it?" Yvette said wistfully.

The maid fidgeted. "We still 'as to comb your 'air, miss."

"I'm sorry. I know it's late. I suppose there's nothing to do but to wear it."

"We all 'as to make sacrifices, miss."

Yvette shot a quick look at her. The maid blanched and seemed about ready to run when Yvette began to laugh. "I think you've been in her ladyship's service far too long. You're beginning to sound like her."

LORD BANCROFT'S high-sprung carriage approached the gates of the house one minute before seven. He looked with pleasure upon the plaque that bore his name and reminded himself to tell Jarvis to see that it was polished on a daily basis.

Laughter burst uncontrolled from his mouth. This evening was sure to be one to remember. He would have given a year of his life to have seen the expression on the women's faces when they arrived home to find the house stripped bare. A mark in his favour at last! The contest to become Yvette's protector had not gone well so far. Indeed, if he failed to make significant progress in the next few days, the odds at White's Club would diminish quickly against him and his self-esteem would suffer a blow.

He pulled out his watch and flicked open the cover. *Aha. Right on time.* Tonight would be the turning point. He had heard about the salon the women were holding on Thursday night. They could hardly entertain without furniture. The owner of the only decent furniture emporium in all of London had promised, for a fee, of course, not to deliver

any goods until the end of the month. Andrew had the ladies right where he wanted them.

The carriage drew to a halt near the steps and Jarvis,
ever alert, opened the door instantly. "Good evening, your
lordship," Jarvis spoke with unusual cordiality.

Andrew was more than a little surprised. "'Evening,
Jarvis. The ladies are expecting me, I believe." He watched
the butler's face with anticipation but there was not the
least flicker of anger or irritation.

"Indeed, sir. I'll inform them that you have arrived.
Would you be so good as to wait in the parlour? I believe
you know the way." He motioned towards the door. "I'm
told the wind is up. Perhaps you would like a brandy to
take away the chill?"

"No, thank you. I'll be quite comfortable."

"Very good, sir," he said, taking Andrew's many-caped
cloak. "Is there anything else?"

Andrew laughed. "No, indeed. Just inform the ladies of
my arrival."

Jarvis nodded and started up the stairs.

Andrew rubbed the chill from his hands and opened the
door to the parlour. The fire would feel good on a night
like this.

The door swung easily inwards. To Andrew's chagrin,
the room was empty. A chandelier blazed from the ceiling
with two dozen tapered candles. On the far side of the
room, the fireplace cast a feeble glow from the embers of
a dying fire. Small as it was, he was drawn towards it. It
proved to be a fatal temptation. He had taken just over a
dozen steps when he realized why the floor shone so
brightly. It had only recently been refinished with some
sort of sticky wax. With each step his slippers felt as if they
were being pulled from his feet. He stood there, legs apart,

undecided whether to advance or retreat. He swore softly. If nothing else, Yvette would pay for this indignity.

Instinct told him that it would be some time before the women were ready to come downstairs. If he returned to the entrance hall, he would have to stand in the cold. Here, at least, he could warm his hands and find a seat on the stone hearth. The damage was already done to his carefully varnished dancing shoes, not to mention *his* beautiful floor. He looked with some compunction at the smeared wood. It would take hours to bring it back to its mirrorlike sheen.

Andrew muttered a curse and giant-stepped his way across the room. *Snick, snick, snick!* With each step, there was a sound which was like a foil pinking his skin. *Demme! What an outrage.* The slippers didn't signify, nor did the floor, he thought as he warmed his hands. What mattered was that the women had scarfed him again. He lowered himself to the stone ledge that fronted the hearth and leaned back. Carefully he lifted his shoes, one by one, and frowned as they pulled free of the floor.

Strategy. That's what he needed. *Think!* he commanded himself. If you go home to change, the chit will have won this bout. The secret was to pretend nothing had happened. He couldn't require Jarvis to clean his shoes, because the butler was in Yvette's employ.

What he needed was one of his own men on the women's staff, a man who was discreet enough to report only to him; a man who would allow him free access to the house whenever he wished. Andrew smiled. It was worth thinking about.

It seemed like an hour later when Lady Udora and Yvette opened the door to the parlour. Lady Udora looked strikingly handsome in a moss-green and gold gown with her hair twisted into a burnished red coil atop her head.

"Ah, there you are, Lord Bancroft. How nice to see you," she said, taking care to remain just outside the room.

He saw over her shoulder that Yvette was standing close behind her. He carefully placed both shoes on the floor and stood. "Good evening, ladies. Would you care to join me by the fire?"

Yvette adjusted a curl behind her ear. "Thank you, no, my lord. I fear we have tarried so long with our hairdresser that we must make our departure at once."

Udora dimpled and cocked her head. "A wise decision. Shall we go, Lord Bancroft?"

He drew a deep breath. "At your service, ladies."

As he hastened towards them, his shoes sounded a steady *snick, snick, snick,* on the shining floor. Both Lady Udora and Yvette felt the only way to hide their amusement was to proceed as quickly as possibly to the door.

CHAPTER SIX

IT SOON BECAME CLEAR to Andrew that he was at a considerable disadvantage matching wits with these two young women. The knowledge ruffled his composure, a fact which further complicated his efforts to gain control. The ladies had already stepped outside when Andrew accepted his cape from Jarvis, noticing at the same time that the somewhat elderly man had a touch of the palsy in his right hand. Andrew patted him on the shoulder.

"Thank you, my good man. You look a bit flaggy. Been a hard day, has it? I suppose you and your wife will be thinking about retiring to a comfortable cottage in the country one day soon."

"Indeed, sir, and it would be nice but I'm a bit too dipped to think on it long. I'll not complain, though. Both her ladyship and the mademoiselle are good to us and the work is not too demanding." He handed Andrew his top hat. "Have a pleasant evening, your lordship."

Andrew was so lost in thought that he mumbled his thanks and went to join the ladies. As soon as he saw them safely ensconced in the carriage with the rug tucked about their knees, he spoke briefly to the driver.

Yvette craned her neck to see what caused the delay, but a moment later Andrew opened the door and climbed in. Lady Udora settled her cape more closely about her neck. "Is something amiss, Lord Bancroft? We don't have a great deal of time to waste."

His features well lit by the glow of the lantern, Andrew cast a charming smile in her direction. "Too true, Lady Udora. Nothing is amiss. I have everything quite under control."

"Indeed? I do hope you are right, my lord." Laughter bubbled beneath the surface of her words as she caught Yvette's eye with a twinkle in her own.

He intercepted the look and tucked it away, vowing to make them pay for their indignities to him and his prized slippers. Twenty minutes later when they arrived at Crampton Pavilion, he wasn't so sure that he could wait for revenge to take its turn. Crampton Pavilion was one of the lesser mansions owned by members of the ton, but it nevertheless boasted a ballroom that easily held two hundred or more guests. The footman then stood to announce them at the head of the short stairway leading down to the sunken ballroom.

"Lord Bancroft. Lady Udora Middlesworth, Mademoiselle Yvette Cordé."

As Andrew stepped forward to hand the ladies down the steps, his shoes stuck to the elegant Moorish rug that graced the landing at the top of the stairs. He stepped quickly with his other foot in an attempt to dislodge the offending slipper, but only succeeded in lifting the rug with both feet.

He was furious. Yvette and Udora tried unsuccessfully to restrain their laughter and the poor footman, at a complete loss, stared saucer-eyed from one to the other. When it appeared that Andrew was going nowhere without the rug flopping at his feet, Udora looked at Yvette and raised an eyebrow.

"Shall we, my dear?"

Yvette inclined her head. "I think it advisable." Without another word they took up a position on either side of him. Given the added weight, Andrew was able to free himself from the rug and make his way amid waves of discreet laughter and a curious *snick, snick, snick,* down the steps to the ballroom. He was soon surrounded by a group of doting mothers who saw him as one of the year's most eligible bachelors. Though it was early in the Season, it was none too soon to start the wheels in motion.

Lady Crampton rushed up to Yvette. "So good of you to come, mademoiselle. Your pianist, Mr. Armbruster, is already here and is waiting for you in the anteroom." She fluttered her fan and touched it to her chin. "I must tell you again what an honour it is to have you sing for us tonight."

"The honour is mine, Lady Crampton," Yvette said, turning her smile on the matron who was remarkable for the cascade of diamonds and rubies that literally covered the top of her high-cut bodice, more than for her quite ordinary features. "You know my companion, Lady Udora," Yvette said.

"Of course." The women inclined their heads to acknowledge each other. "Lady Udora and my eldest daughter came out in the same Season," she said, her voice guarded.

Udora regarded her with a smile. "Ah yes, so many years ago. Over ten, isn't it? And how is our little Genevieve?"

"Very well. Married to the German count, you know, and expecting their third child. A true love match, it was."

"Lovely. And your son? Rupert was his name, I believe. Is he married?"

Lady Crampton visibly panicked. She blinked and began to fan herself in an agitated manner. "Yes, Rupert. He...ah...No, Lady Udora, he is not yet wed, but he is quite unavailable. He is, I assure you, betrothed to a lovely young heiress from Yorkshire way. The agreement has already been signed and arrangements have been made for their wedding.''

Yvette saw the sparkle in Udora's eyes and prepared for the worst. Udora dimpled. ''Why, Lady Crampton, I do so wish I had got to him first.''

Lady Crampton blanched. ''Pity. Well, you must excuse me. I have guests to attend to.'' She turned to Yvette. ''I've already announced that you will entertain shortly. Whenever you are ready you may begin.'' Without waiting for her response, she scurried off to join a gathering of débutantes at the far side of the room.

Yvette started towards the anteroom with Udora at her side. ''Is it true? Were you really attracted to Rupert Crampton?''

Udora stopped dead in her tracks. ''I consider that an insult above half. Have you met Rupert Crampton? He's twenty-and-five if he's a day. When he dines he wipes his hands on his pantaloons and sucks his teeth with his mouth open. And those are his good points.''

Yvette laughed. ''Then why did you say what you did?''

''Why?'' she asked, taking Yvette's arm as they continued on their way. ''Because the poor woman suffers enough having a son such as he. Why not let her have a moment of pleasure? Besides, she had yet to present you with her, ah...shall we call it a gesture of goodwill, for your concert tonight. We certainly can't afford to antagonize her.''

Yvette knew better than to argue that point. The second payment on the house was due within the month. And now there was furniture to be replaced. But she couldn't allow herself to dwell on her problems before the concert. It was important that she smile and act as if her only worldly concern was to entertain the lords and ladies of the ton.

It wasn't an easy task. From the curtained doorway leading onto the small stage, she could see the dancers floating to the music of a string quartet who were seated in a railed box at the far right beyond the stage.

The ballroom was aglitter with diamonds and jewels brought to life by the flickering light from ten crystal chandeliers. Gowns of satin and lace made brilliant islands of colour in a sea of white-satin knee breeches. Near the potted palm trees by the walls, eager mothers watched their daughters flirt with any and every man between the ages of eighteen and seventy-five.

Yvette's gaze was drawn to the dancers and though she hated to admit it, she knew it was Lord Bancroft for whom she was searching. Surprisingly, he did not appear to be engaged in the lively quadrille.

Peering around Yvette for her own view, Udora apparently read Yvette's mind. "I hardly think he'll risk dancing, Yvette. Not unless he first removes his footwear. The sound would drown out the music."

Yvette grinned. "That was a cruel thing we did."

"Nonsense. He did it to himself." She stepped away from the curtain. "You look lovely. The russet gown is perfect with your fair skin. Strange, though, it makes your hair look more brown than black." She shrugged. "No matter. I've spoken with Mr. Armbruster and he has agreed to look after you until you've finished with your songs. In the meantime," she batted long lashes, "I plan to circulate. It's been a while since I've scouted the marriage market to see what it has to offer." She did a graceful pirouette. "Tell me, do I look presentable?"

"You look beautiful. But I would advise you not to flirt with just anyone, Lady Udora. You might find yourself betrothed before the evening's half done."

Udora peeked over the lace edging the top of her fan. "Interesting thought. Excuse me, my dear. There is one more set before your concert begins. I must fill my card."

Yvette joined Mr. Armbruster at the table where he was going over the music before their appearance on stage. He seemed slightly more nervous than usual.

"Are you anxious, mademoiselle?" he enquired, pushing his spectacles back on his nose.

Yvette nodded. "As always. The last song worries me. I sometimes forget the words and the appoggiaturas are difficult for me to execute so quickly."

"But the increased tempo is necessary to create the feeling of fairies frolicking in the woods. That is the whole idea of 'Woodsprites and Elves Dancing on a Summer's Eve,' you know."

"I know. I will try but you must be ready to save me if I miss a note or two."

"You never do, mademoiselle. Come." He stood and shuffled the music in the proper order. "Are you ready? The set is nearly over and Lady Crampton is waiting to introduce you."

Yvette straightened her gown, fluffed her hair and settled the amber pendant that graced the top of her bodice. The room quieted immediately when Lady Crampton stepped up to the dais. It was as if the guests had waited all evening for this precise moment, and indeed, such was the truth. Near the centre of the room she saw Udora smiling from the arm of the Swedish Ambassador and her spirits lifted. After the brief introduction, Lady Crampton touched a hand to her glittering bosom.

''Mademoiselle Cordé will begin this evening's concert with an old favourite, 'Milkmaids of Devonshire.''' A murmur of approval swept across the room and Yvette clasped her hands at her waist and nodded to Mr. Armbruster to begin. The introduction was barely long enough to give Yvette a chance to search the room for Lord Bancroft but he was nowhere to be seen. Was he so angry that he had deserted them? Not likely. He had his faults but one could hardly accuse him of being a spoil-sport. Above all, she admired his sense of humour, even when he was the butt of the joke. Still... where was he?

Somehow, she managed to get through the first song. While they waited for the applause to end before beginning the opening bars of the 'The Mermaid's Lament,' Yvette saw Lord Bancroft enter the ballroom with a débutante dressed in a flowing white gown. The chit clung to his arm like sticktights to a pair of wool stockings. And she was *sans* chaperon, too! The nerve of him! He was nothing but a rakehell and an adventurer.

Realizing suddenly that Mr. Armbruster had repeated the last three bars of her introduction, Yvette felt the heat rise in her face. She looked over at him and the slight frown that creased his forehead was set-down enough to maintain her concentration throughout the rest of the concert.

The audience was generous with its applause and would have kept her on stage for another hour, but Mr. Armbruster stood and bowed, a sure signal that there were to be no more encores. When they returned to the anteroom he dropped the music on the table and spoke. ''A word with you, mademoiselle.''

Yvette was contrite. ''Forgive me, Mr. Armbruster. I know I was foolish to let my mind wander. Thank you for coming to my rescue.''

"I only wanted to say that you performed well despite the one small incident. I daresay that no one except you noticed it."

"Thank you. I..." She was about to say more when she sensed someone watching her and turned to see Lord Bancroft standing in the doorway. This time he was quite alone.

He bowed. "My compliments, Mademoiselle Yvette. Each time I hear you sing I marvel that your voice is so pure."

She gave him an appraising look. "I hadn't thought you would bother with such trivial entertainment, my lord. You seem to find so many fascinating diversions."

He lifted an eyebrow. "I take it then that you were watching me when you missed the opening bars of your song?"

Her face flamed. "Indeed not. I was merely trying to...to catch my breath."

"Is there a difference? I think not."

"You are conceited above half. If you will excuse me, I wish to join the party." She made as if to pass through the doorway but he successfully blocked her exit. "May I?" he asked, offering her his arm.

She seemed to have little choice in the matter, so sighing, she placed her gloved hand on his sleeve. "Please feel free to rejoin the débutantes, my lord." She spoke loudly because the clack and gabble of the assemblage of people all trying to outdo each other, was nearly deafening. "As for myself," she continued, "I am engaged for the next dance." She smiled wickedly. "I'm sure you would prefer conversation in lieu of making a fool of yourself on the dance floor."

He looked appalled. "Are you casting aspersions on my footwork?"

"Never. You are an accomplished dancer, a fact that I freely admit. Tonight, however, the sound of your shoes would likely set the musicians' teeth on edge."

He took her hands in his and held her captive. "Or perhaps they may think it is you trying once again to catch your breath." He transferred her hand to his other palm and held both of hers quite easily, neither crushing them in his grip, nor yet allowing her to escape. With his free hand he signalled to the musicians and they began to play a lilting Viennese waltz.

"Mademoiselle?"

Yvette gasped. "I can't. it would be most improper. I've already promised Mr. Lindsey."

"Mr. Lindsey has made a sudden departure. He asked me to present his apologies." He swept her onto the floor and whirled in time to the music.

"You are a cad, sir. What have you done to him?"

"Nothing, short of complimenting him on the size of his feet."

Yvette stole a glance at the floor. "Fie! You've pinched his shoes."

"Traded, if you must know. And the Grubstreet poet was pleased to oblige."

"You threatened him, then."

"Privilege of rank, of course, but the man was no fool. He knew enough to barter." Andrew pulled her a bit closer while they executed an elaborate spin. "However, I thought this dance worth the price."

When the waltz was finished, Yvette caught his gaze. "You bribed him?"

"Pray why not?" He held her at arm's length. "Don't look at me as if I were an unprincipled backhander. The money I gave him will keep him in cheroots for six months. It astounds me that Lord Crampton would stoop to invite such a mushroom to his party simply because he's published a book of verse."

Too late he realized what he had said and how Yvette might interpret it. She, on the other hand, appeared not to have heard. She was watching a man on the far side of the room: a servant, wearing the Crampton livery but appearing singularly awkward with the tray he was attempting to balance on one arm.

It wasn't the first time Andrew had seen Yvette apparently entranced by a strange man. He scowled. What was it that caught her eye? Was it the width of the man's shoulders, the ruthless slant of his mouth? Or was it something else? Did she know the man? It occurred to him suddenly that Yvette was caught between the worlds of service and Society and he had little knowledge of what went on in her life when they were apart.

He caught a drift of her scent, a mixture of lilac and roses, and he made up his mind that he would learn everything about her.

Yvette had seen the man before, she was certain of it. But where? Where? Was it at the Whyteside ball? No. It went further back than that. He never looked directly at her, but when she turned unexpectedly she caught a glimpse of his eyes studying her face before they slid away.

Andrew gripped her fingers where they rested on his hand. She snapped her head back to look at him and he smiled. "That's better. Good manners dictate that you give me your full attention when I dance with you."

"My apologies, Lord Bancroft, but one can hardly expect correct behaviour from a servant. Or have you forgotten that I was only recently an upstairs maid at Berrington House?"

"So you did hear my unforgivable remark after all? I do most heartily beg your forgiveness, Yvette. There is no comparison between you and the fellow who sold me his shoes. A poet he is, but he keeps the fact well hidden beneath his bear-garden exterior. The rumours about him are unfit for your tender ears."

"And you have not heard the rumours about me? That I am the daughter of gypsies or the illegitimate daughter of a naval hero?"

He laughed. "They are of no consequence. Beautiful women are always talked about. What concerns me is what I see with my own eyes. You, my dear, have the beauty and bearing of a queen and the voice of an angel."

She ignored his obvious attempt at flummery. Flattery meant nothing to her, but gossip did. "I have no wish to be the subject of additional rumours, sir, so I suggest you release me. The music has ceased."

Lord Bancroft had the decency to look taken aback. His expression brought a smile to Yvette's lips. He grinned. "Since I've had but one dance tonight, thanks to the unfortunate condition of my shoes, I thought to make it last as long as possible." He bowed. "My gratitude for an enchanting waltz, mademoiselle. May I escort you to your companion?"

She dropped a curtsy. "Yes, thank you, my lord." Yvette would have enjoyed another waltz with him, but to permit it would severely compromise her reputation. To her surprise, he lingered at her side to share a lively discussion with Udora, the handsome young Earl of Vassey, and a growing entourage of listeners. It would have been perfect if she had not felt it necessary to look constantly over her shoulder to see if she were being watched. As it was, the curiously inept servant had apparently vanished some time during the waltz.

During the carriage ride home Andrew leaned forward with his hands on his knees. His voice still held the excitement of the evening. "Ladies, I must thank you for permitting me the honour of escorting you to the soirée. The two of you were the toasts of the party."

Udora tucked her hands inside her muff and snuggled down into the folds of her cape. "I trust you will be joining us for our Thursday evening salon, Lord Bancroft."

"The King's guards could not keep me away." He grinned. "That is, if you promise that your house will be ready in time."

Yvette, remembering that he had taken away their furniture, said with more confidence than she felt, "We will have seating for everyone, I assure you."

"I was referring to the condition of your floor, mademoiselle. It would be a pity if the wax somehow failed to dry in time."

"Do not concern yourself. I am quite capable of running my own household."

"Of course. However I deem it appropriate to keep an eye on my investment. You do remember that the second instalment is due within a week's time?"

Udora reached over to pat his arm. "How could we forget? Have no fear. The money will be there on the prescribed day."

"Indeed."

It was impossible to miss the disappointment in his voice. Yvette slanted a look across at Udora, a look that said much more than words could ever convey.

Once they arrived back at the house Andrew made it clear that he would accept an invitation to come in for a late supper. Udora obviously would have enjoyed his company, but Yvette dismissed the idea by saying that she and Udora were exhausted and wished to retire early.

Later, in the library, Yvette confronted Udora. "What did you mean by telling Lord Bancroft that we would have the money ready in two days? If I use my remaining funds, there'll be nothing left to live on and I can't accept money from you."

"Pistachions! I have no intention of giving you the money, though if you truly needed it..." She laughed and dumped the contents of her reticule on the table. "*Voilà!* Have you ever seen anything so beautifully vulgar?"

Yvette gasped. "Emeralds! Are they real?" she asked, picking up the heavy gold bracelet that was set with three stunning emeralds, the largest she had ever seen.

"Real? I should hope so! The bracelet is a tribute to your lovely voice from Lord and Lady Crampton."

"How generous of them."

"Ah yes, though we both know this obscenity must have been in their vault for generations. It is far too ugly to wear."

"It is, isn't it? How much do you think it will fetch at the jewellers?"

"Not enough as it is, but I know a broker who will reset the emeralds and make three pendants that will bring us twice as much as the bracelet would have. He will advance us enough tomorrow to meet your next payment with sufficient money left over to run the house for several months. In the meantime, use the money you have on hand to keep the constable from the door."

"And what about furniture?" Yvette said. "It is far too late to tell everyone we have invited for Thursday that the salon has been cancelled."

"Leave it to me." Udora tossed her cap of red-gold curls. "If we have no chairs our guests can dance instead of sitting down. Perhaps we can hire a dance master to teach them the latest reel."

Yvette started to protest until she realized that Udora was only half serious. She laughed. "You are impossible.

We couldn't afford musicians and Lord Bancroft has taken my pianoforte along with the other furniture.''

Udora shrugged. "Tomorrow is time enough for that." She called her cats and they came scurrying out from under the furniture and draperies. Sinbad, however, who always slept in the wing chair near the fireplace stretched and jumped down. "Come, boys. Time for beddie-byes." She tucked them under one arm and over one shoulder as she started for the stairs, then looked back at Yvette. "Don't worry. Tomorrow I'll visit Bond Street and see what they have to offer."

Yvette was too tired to argue. Before she went upstairs she opened the door to the parlour and surveyed the shiny floor. A few spots remained to mark Andrew's passage across the room. Even though the damage was temporary, she felt a twinge of guilt at having been responsible for it. The smell of wax lay heavily on the air and when she bent to test its dryness, her fingers detected a slight stickiness. "Fie!" she said, under her breath. "Maybe he was right. Maybe it will never dry completely. And wouldn't he love that!"

CHAPTER SEVEN

THE NEXT DAY, however, presented a whole new set of problems. Yvette woke with a start long before her usual time. Whether she had been dreaming or whether she had heard a real sound she could not be certain, but she thought she had heard a horse approach the house and make its way round to the servants' gate. She lay quietly waiting to be summoned by her maid if something was amiss, but when no message arrived, Yvette drifted back to sleep.

The problems began when she came downstairs to breakfast. Jarvis and his wife approached her with a profound show of reluctance.

"I beg your pardon, Mademoiselle Cordé," Jarvis said, clutching the ends of his jacket. "We must talk with you."

Yvette carefully placed her cup on the saucer. "Yes, Jarvis. What is it?"

He stood stiffly, hands pressed against his thighs as if he needed contact with something solid. He looked over at his wife and she nodded. "The truth is, miss, that my wife and I have decided to give notice."

Yvette was astounded. "You're leaving? I can't believe it. Jarvis, Clara? Were you so unhappy in my employ? Has someone offered you a better position?"

"No indeed, miss. Both you and her ladyship have been good to us. The truth is, we have the chance to buy the little cottage we've had our sights on for some years now. In

Yorkshire it is, with room for a little garden and a cow or two, and maybe even a goat.''

"This is rather sudden, isn't it? Does Lady Udora know? She was, after all, your employer before you came here.''

"Ay, 'tis true it's sudden enough, but none too soon. Neither my missus nor I am getting any younger. We just couldn't say no, miss.''

An alarm bell sounded in her head. "You couldn't say no? Then someone is making it possible for you to retire?''

Jarvis looked edgy. "That he is, miss, but I'm sworn to secrecy. We'll be leaving today.''

"So soon?" Yvette was appalled. "Not even a day's notice?''

"Those were the conditions, miss. The owner doesn't want the cottage left vacant.''

"I see. I hope you can explain all this to Lady Udora.''

Lady Udora sailed into the dining room in a cloud of lavender cologne. "Explain what to Lady Udora?''

Yvette pushed her chair away from the table and stood. "It seems that Jarvis and Clara are leaving us today to retire to a cottage in Yorkshire.''

"Pistachions, you say! It can't be true. Tell me it isn't, Jarvis. You can't be deserting us in our time of need. We have guests coming tomorrow night.''

"I'm most regretful, your ladyship. We'll be leaving before tea-time," he said, then repeated the information he had given to Yvette.

Udora was miffed. "And just who is your benevolent friend, pray tell?''

Yvette sat down. "They are sworn to secrecy but I'll venture to say that Lord Bancroft is behind this.''

Jarvis blanched. "I beg forgiveness, miss. I can truthfully say that Lord Bancroft never spoke on the subject."

"Indeed. Then perhaps you can tell me the name of the rider who called at the servants' door just after dawn?"

Clara answered in her soft voice, at the same time knotting her handkerchief between her fingers. "'E was a messenger, 'e was, from the firm o' Dobbney, Fitch and Stern. 'Twas 'e what put the deed in our 'ands. That's all we know, miss."

Udora attempted to question them again but the effort proved fruitless and she dismissed them with a wave of her hand.

"There's more to this than we've heard so far," she said, taking her plate to the buffet for a serving of pilchard, fried potatoes and soft, buttery scones.

"It was Andrew Waverly, Lord Bancroft. I know it as surely as I know that rabbits beget rabbits."

"Of course. Who else would stoop so low?" Udora laughed helplessly. "Unless of course it is Andrew's mother. Alicia Waverly is desperate to discredit you. Did you know that she was watching you like a vulture last night while you were singing?"

"No. I didn't see her. Why would she want to put me in disfavour?"

"Don't be a ninnyhammer. She fears an alliance between you and Andrew, of course." Udora reached over and touched Yvette on the hand. "Now don't be offended, Yvette, but Lady Bancroft is a high stickler and obsessed with preserving the blood lines. It would devastate her if Andrew did not marry her choice."

"Marriage is not uppermost in his mind, nor mine, suffice it to say."

"But it needs must be. Andrew is no longer a callow youth, my dear. With no one to succeed him the title will be lost. Take my word for it, Andrew will marry within two years or her ladyship will make him regret it."

"He is no weakling. He will do as he pleases."

"I grant you that he is stronger than most men, but when it comes to his heritage, he's been well trained. He will do what he must to preserve the line. Take my advice and play your cards well."

Yvette was appalled. "Are you saying that I should trap him into marriage?"

"Why not? You could hardly do better. You could otherwise end up with a protector, or worse yet, as an old maid with no one to warm your bed."

"My bed is quite warm enough, thank you."

"Hmmph. There is none so blind as she who will not see."

"I'm quite capable of taking care of myself. I have, ever since the day..." She stopped abruptly.

Udora looked curious. "You were saying?"

Yvette flushed. "Since the day I left France."

Udora gave her a look that said she recognized the attempted subterfuge but chose to ignore it. "Someday, Yvette, I'd like very much for you to tell me about it."

Yvette rose abruptly from her chair. "Another time, perhaps. Later today we must try to find another butler and housekeeper in time for our Thursday salon."

"Impossible. It could take days, weeks even, to find decent help."

"Then we must accept what we can get. In the meantime, there is something I must do." She turned sharply and strode towards the kitchen stairs. Twenty minutes later, armed with hammer and chisel, she marched purposefully down the front drive to the entrance gate.

LATER THAT MORNING, Andrew, in fine good humour, tooled his curricle towards the entrance to Waverly Lodge. The tune he whistled stopped abruptly when he saw Yvette swinging a hammer at the gatepost with all the vigour of a stone cutter.

He pulled in alongside her and dragged the horse to a dead stop. "Cease that at once! What, by all that's holy, are you doing? Have you gone mad?"

She turned, a chillingly sweet smile frozen on her face. "Good morning, Lord Bancroft. If you are here for your next instalment, I fear you must return later in the day."

He jumped the bushes that separated them and grabbed the hammer from her hand. "God's blood! It's too late. You've done it now. You, Mademoiselle Cordé, are no lady."

"*Sacré bleu!* You have made that quite obvious, my lord, in your treatment of me." Yvette handed him the heavy, bronzed plaque that bore his family name. "My apologies, but I fear it was difficult to remove. There is a small piece missing on the upper edge."

He held the bronze plate out in front of him. "A piece missing? It looks as if someone has taken an enormous bite out of it."

"Just so. The chisel slipped. It occurred to me that I might leave the task to you, but I was afraid you might refuse to do it."

"You could place a wager on that!" He stood there staring, first at the ruined plaque and then at the bald spot on the lichen-covered gate stone.

Yvette hadn't realized it meant so much to him. For a brief moment she was overcome by a deep sense of regret, but it didn't last long. He flung the plate to the ground and strode back to his carriage.

"I warrant you'll be sorry for this, mademoiselle. If your payment isn't ready by tea-time, I'll have the bailiff sent round to evict you before you can flick your fan." He snapped the whip at his horse and it reared in a sharp turn that spun the two-wheeled carriage in a semicircle.

Yvette held her breath. She had never seen him so angry...nor so breathtakingly intriguing. She recognized and understood that certain look in his eyes. She was French, after all. Instinct told her that his anger was not entirely directed towards her most recent actions, but had more to do with his failure to get his way in other specific areas. If that were indeed true, he could expect to be vexed for a long time, for she had no intention of becoming his mistress.

Perhaps now he would give up and let her live her life without his constant intervention. But even as the thought occurred to her, she hoped it wasn't true. He had been gone less than a minute and already she missed him. Whenever he was nearby there was a special radiance in the air. Udora was right: the excitement that the presence of a certain man could generate did add something to an otherwise dull life. At any rate, he would certainly return late in the afternoon to collect his money.

As it turned out, it was Mr. Umbarton, Lord Bancroft's solicitor, who arrived to claim the payment. He was a dapper little man, short, with a chiselled moustache which moved when he breathed. His suit was of the finest cloth from a Mount street tailor, a fact that belied his reputation for being clutch-fisted. Seeing how he counted the money three times before offering a receipt, Yvette concluded that he was a miser in relation to others and not to himself.

"How does it happen that you have come instead of Lord Bancroft?" Yvette asked, in spite of her determination not to.

"His lordship was in a bit of a humour, if I may be so bold. He didn't look well at all, mademoiselle. A touch of indigestion, perhaps."

"Perhaps. May I offer you a cup of tea, Mr. Umbarton, or a glass of sherry?"

He hesitated, then declined, apparently having seen the censure in Udora's eyes. "I appreciate your hospitality, mademoiselle, but I still have several calls to make."

Yvette clucked her tongue. "I truly sympathize with you. It must have been a long day for you, what with your crack-of-dawn visit to my house this morning. I severely chastised Jarvis for not serving you breakfast."

"Thank you kindly but I ate before I—" He stopped and his mouth dropped open. "That is, I..."

Udora slapped her hand on the table. "Do be considerate enough not to prevaricate further, Mr. Umbarton. We are well aware that it is Lord Bancroft who arranged an early retirement for my domestics."

Her words flattened his face for a moment but he managed to pull himself to his full, if insignificant height. "I'll neither confirm nor deny it, my lady."

"There is no need. Now if you have no further business, we shall be pleased to see you to the door...since our butler is occupied in packing."

He had the grace to depart as quickly as he had come.

Yvette picked up the receipt and folded it carefully into an envelope which she marked for identification. "I was quite sure it was Andrew who bought off Jarvis and his wife but I truly didn't want to believe it. Now there seems to be no doubt."

"Lord Bancroft will stop at nothing to get his way. He knew we planned to entertain on Thursday evening. He wants us to go to him, cap in hand. His strategy is flawless."

"Then we mustn't let him win," Yvette said.

"Up until now I would have agreed with you, but we can hardly entertain without a cook and a butler. The butler we could manage, but a cook..."

"It's not as if we planned to serve dinner. I thought perhaps some wine and French pastries."

"French pastries. Surely you jest, Yvette. It takes a specialist to make decent pastry."

"I could bake them, Lady Udora. Our chef taught... I mean, in the place where I worked when I lived in Paris, I learned the art of pastry-making."

Udora gave her a quizzical look. "Is that so? All right. This is what we'll do. I'll see to getting some chairs for the drawing room. You take charge of the refreshments."

"But you can't possibly visit the shops unescorted."

"Pistachions, Yvette! I may be close to your own age, but one would hardly consider me a maiden still in need of a dragon. While I am in town I shall also make it known at the agency that we are in need of a butler and cook. And by the way, do forgo calling me Lady Udora. It makes me feel so *old*. After all, there is but five or six years' difference in our ages."

Yvette suppressed a laugh. Five or six years, indeed. She was a good ten years younger than Udora. But later, on her way to the kitchen to make an inventory of the supplies, it occurred to her that she often felt as if Udora, with her penchant for enjoying life, was the younger and that she, herself, was the one about to kiss thirty.

Save for the cats, who clamoured to be fed, the kitchen was quite empty when Yvette went downstairs to inspect the pantry. Ulysses and his twin brother Odysseus wrapped themselves about her legs until she had little choice but to fill their bowls with milk. Prometheus and Telemachus, with their noses tucked under their paws, were curled up in their basket like two reddish-brown balls of fur. Sinbad was nowhere to be seen but Yvette guessed that he would be enthroned on the Queen Anne chair in the library. When he wasn't exploring he was usually fast asleep there in his favourite chair.

Yvette watched fascinated as the two tabbies lapped the milk. The tips of their tails moved from side to side in unison as if they were directing a company of musicians. She bent down to scratch Prom's head and he arched his back against her hand, somehow contriving to purr while still drinking.

Through the open door abovestairs she heard the or-molu clock chime the hour and she sighed. Wasting precious moments like these would hardly get the pastry made. She washed her hands and began assembling the butter, flour, cream, and various ingredients she would need during the next few hours. In the back of the pantry she discovered dusty but still palatable jars of currant and raspberry jelly. There was an ample supply of chunks of sugar in a tightly covered crockery jar. Everything she needed was there, including a discarded apron that encircled her waist with room to spare. The fire in the grate warmed the cavernous kitchen with a cheerful glow and all that remained was to discover if she could remember what Monsieur Villechaise had taught her.

It was over three hours later when Yvette began to worry that Udora had not returned. While another batch of pastry was chilling in the cold room, Yvette ran upstairs to speak to Udora's abigail. But no information was forthcoming. Maggie McGee had not seen Udora since she left in the carriage to buy chairs for the drawing room earlier that afternoon.

Yvette tried to hide her uneasiness with a smile. "I suppose she is all right. Lady Udora is quite capable, I'm sure."

"Yes, miss. She often visits the shops unescorted."

"I wonder, Maggie. Would you be so good as to answer the door, should anyone knock this afternoon? You know, of course, that Mr. and Mrs. Jarvis are leaving us today?"

"Yes, miss. 'Cept I can't 'ear so good from all the way up 'ere."

"Then perhaps you could take your work downstairs for the rest of the afternoon. You have the lace to repair on Lady Udora's cap, I believe, and the hem to sew up on the yellow watered silk." She saw a frown flicker across the girl's wide brow and suspected that Maggie objected to taking orders from her.

Yvette turned at the doorway. "And when you're finished you might come down to the kitchen for a cup of tea and a piece of French pastry."

That seemed to satisfy her. She dropped a curtsy and said she would see to it at once.

Another hour passed. A strange carriage came to escort Mr. and Mrs. Jarvis to their cottage in the country. They seemed somewhat relieved to take their departure without having to face Lady Udora for the last time. Yvette wished them well despite the inconvenience they had caused her.

She was in the middle of spreading butter between the layers of dough when Maggie popped her head into the kitchen. "Excuse me, miss. The new butler and 'is wife is waitin' in the 'allway. I didn't know where to put 'em, considerin' there's no chairs left 'cept what's in the library."

"The new butler? Are you sure that's what he said?"

"And the new cook. It's wot 'e said a'right."

"Hmm. I suppose Lady Udora hired them. I had no idea she would find anyone this quickly. Very well. Send them to the library. I'll see them as soon as the raspberry tarts are out of the oven."

Yvette felt as if a load had been lifted from her shoulders. The Thursday salon was obviously very important to Udora and it would have been regrettable if their first attempt at entertaining had turned disadventurous. So many guests had been invited. Of course it was unlikely that more than a few would appear. With the Season just beginning, anyone with two coins to rub together would be sending out invitations to the members of the haut ton. It was somewhat presumptuous to assume that the denizens of Society would forgo a palace just to spend the evening at her large, if comparably humble, abode. And it was just as well, she thought, grimacing as she took the tarts from the oven and set them to cool. If Udora failed to find decent furnishings for the drawing room they would be the laughing-stock of London.

Doffing the apron, she pushed back a curl beneath her mob cap and started towards the stairs. On second thought she pulled off the cap and put on her best lady-of-the-manor smile before receiving the newly hired couple in the library. Appearances must be kept up, as Lady Margaret was so fond of saying.

Thinking of the countess reminded Yvette of Lady Emily, who must be very near her lying-in time. Would they have the boy she so badly wanted, or the girl that his lordship was said to favour? Suffice it to say that they would be delighted with either one.

When Yvette entered the library, both the new butler and his wife stood. "Good afternoon," Yvette said, quickly taking in their appearance. "I am Mademoiselle Cordé. And you are?"

He bowed. "Douglas McMasters, mademoiselle. This is my wife, Mary. She cooks and keeps house. 'Tis pleased we are to be coming into your employ."

"Very well. You understand the conditions and you find them satisfactory?"

"Yes, indeed."

Yvette studied his lean frame, neatly combed hair, and carefully pared fingernails. He was the picture of what a butler should be. Mary was a findy woman with a round face and merry blue eyes that bespoke a jolly disposition. While they were not young, neither of them appeared old enough to consider retirement for several years to come. That in itself was a blessing.

Yvette drew a deep breath. "We are expecting a large number of guests tomorrow evening, not for dinner, you understand. I wonder if it would be an imposition for you to begin work by tomorrow afternoon?"

Mary McMasters put her hands to her chin and laughed. "We hoped to settle in and begin work today, miss, if it ain't too soon. The mister left the bags at the servant's gate."

"Today? Why, that would be marvellous. If you'll come with me, I'll show you to your rooms."

After she had left them to unpack, it occurred to Yvette that she had failed to ask about their previous experience, but of course Udora would have questioned them at length. They were, in fact, almost too good to be true, Yvette decided. But leave it to Udora. She had a talent for providing easy answers to difficult problems.

By the time Lady Udora finally arrived home, McMasters was in uniform and standing at the ready to answer the door. Coming downstairs to meet her, Yvette overheard Udora instruct the butler as to the disposition of the bundles she had left piled in the carriage.

Her face was wreathed in smiles when she saw Yvette. "Good girl! You've been the busy one, now haven't you?"

"Oh? You can smell the tarts, I suppose. I've baked enough to feed an army." She followed Udora to the library where she collapsed into a chair. Yvette offered her a glass of sherry.

"You deserve it after everything you've accomplished. The McMasters seem to be a delightful pair."

Udora stretched her legs out in front of her. "Yes. Aren't they, though. Wherever did you find them?"

"Where did *I* find them? I thought you hired them."

"On the contrary. I stopped at two agencies and neither of them could provide us with help for at least three weeks."

"But that's impossible. Where did they come from?"

"No doubt one of the friends I spoke to sent them by; I shall certainly find out in due course. In the meantime we are desperate for help for the party. If they perform well and are trustworthy, they will suffice for the present. Besides, the butler looks to be a decent sort. He has exceedingly good legs."

Yvette laughed. "I'm sure his wife thinks so. Tell me, did you have any success finding chairs for our party tomorrow night?"

Udora rose quickly. "In a manner of speaking. I think they will serve quite well. But let me tell you all about it later. For now, I must retire to my room. I feel as if I have tramped from one end of London to the other. Trust me, Yvette. The party will be the talk of London."

Before she had a chance to pursue the subject Udora left. Yvette stood in the middle of the room until, belatedly, she followed Udora into the hallway and watched her climb the stairs.

McMasters came up to her while she was standing there and asked what to do with the mound of bundles he had brought in from the carriage.

"What are they?" she asked.

"I've no idea, mademoiselle, but they appear to be cloth of some kind."

Yvette lifted the paper from one end to reveal what appeared to be yards and yards of silk in shades of pale lavender, pink, and misty yellow. Another bundle was twin to the first and a third package, longer and thinner than the two, contained gold tasseled ropes of considerable length.

"What on earth?"

"There's more, mademoiselle. Three big bundles. Rugs, they are. Turkish, I think."

"Sacré bleu!" she whispered, then leaned against a carved pillar and pressed her fingers to her temples. Whatever could the woman have been thinking of? *Udora Middlesworth,* Yvette said to herself, *I think you have finally curdled the soup.*

CHAPTER EIGHT

IT TOOK YVETTE less than ten seconds to climb the stairs and knock on Udora's bedchamber door—ten seconds in which her mood deteriorated from puzzled to irritated. "Udora, I must talk to you."

"Not now, sweetling. I must rest for a while. My feet feel like two overripe plums. Why don't you take a nap, too, and be fresh for this evening? I'll send Maggie to your room with a pot of chamomile tea."

Experience told Yvette there was no point in arguing. When Udora was ready to talk she would talk. As for herself, her head was splitting more from nerves than from the heat in the kitchen. A rest could only improve her disposition.

She had hardly reached her room when Maggie appeared with the pot of tea already set to steep. The faintly bitter drink did its work. Yvette had no sooner put her head to her pillow than she was lost in a dreamless sleep.

It was nearly three hours later when she arose, appalled that she had slept so long. She frowned. Her mouth had a fuzzy taste, as if she had been sleeping for a week. When she went to Udora's room, the abigail was straightening the bed.

"Where is she, Maggie? Pray don't tell me that she has gone out again."

"I couldna' say, miss. But an hour ago I 'eard the new butler and two draymen fetching some boxes and sech to the drawing room.'' She grinned. ''Uffin' and puffin' they was, too.''

''Thank you, Maggie.''

Something was going on, something that Udora was reluctant to admit to. And Yvette was determined to find out. But nothing could have prepared her for what she saw when she opened the door to the drawing room.

The large room, which a few hours earlier had been nearly empty of furniture, now looked like a scene from *Ten Nights in a Turkish Harem*. Yards of silken draperies were strung from the chandeliers to various points along the ornamental coping where walls were joined to the ceiling. The least breath of air wafted the silk to and fro like a sky filled with pastel-coloured clouds. The movement in turn caused the tinkle of hidden bells, a sound so light and delicate that for a moment, Yvette thought she had imagined it.

Across the floor dozens of Turkish rugs were scattered between mounds of pillows large enough to seat half a dozen people each, and close together enough that adjoining groups could share the conversation. Black lacquered tables with squat, round legs completed the groupings. Some of the tables held candles set in fat globes of multicoloured glass.

''Mon Dieu!'' Yvette murmured, holding onto the doorway for support. ''What have they done to my house?''

''Is that you, Yvette?'' Udora asked, coming out from behind one of a dozen or more clusters of potted palm trees. ''Ah, yes. Come in. Come in. Don't just stand there. Isn't it delightful?''

Yvette slowly let out her breath. ''Delightful? *Decadent* would be more appropriate.''

"Precisely. Just what I had in mind. A little like a Turkish harem, wouldn't you say? Only perhaps a trifle more tasteful."

"Udora, much as I hate to prick your bubble...don't you think this setting is a little bizarre for our Thursday salon?"

"Bizarre is an apt word. I warrant that everyone in London will be talking about us," Udora said with obvious pride.

"The question is, what will they be saying? I'm not sure we should expose ourself to ridicule in an effort to curry Society's favour."

"Trust me, Yvette. We are going to take London Society by the scruff of its neck and give it a good shake. And all in perfectly good taste, I might add."

"That is comforting to hear but I wonder if anyone will believe it."

"Good heavens! Did you think we were going to sponsor a Bacchanalian revel?"

"The thought crossed my mind."

"I consider that an insult to my character. Surely, Yvette, you must know by now that although I may stretch the rules a wee bit, I never go beyond the bounds of propriety. We shall entertain the cream of London Society as well as some of the most prominent intellectuals."

"I didn't mean to besmirch your character, Udora. I know that you would not deliberately compromise our reputations. I simply wonder if perhaps you haven't gone a bit too far. You must admit that the room does take some getting used to."

She dimpled. "Our guests will love it. And if some of them also happen to be the most eligible bachelors London has to offer," she said airily, "then our investment will be worth every penny. I assure you, Yvette, that no man between the ages of eighteen and sixty will turn down an invitation.''

"Just where did you discover this, er...I'm at a loss to know what to call it.''

" 'Treasure' will suffice. It came straight from the hold of the *Raza Dey,* a distressed Turkish sailing ship whose cargo was consigned to a linen-draper. Fortunately for me, he was the brother of my third husband. The moment I saw the pillows I knew they were the answer to our prayers. Eustace, dear man that he is, included the miniature cymbals at no charge. And these,'' she said, bringing out a heavily laden tray, ''are the crowning touch.''

"Candles?''

"More than just candles, Yvette. Wait.'' She placed the tray on a table and ignited a gypsy match. The odour of sulphur was almost immediately replaced by the subtle fragrance of cloves and exotic gums of frankincense, and a heady flowerlike perfume which Yvette was unable to identify.

She groaned. "Incense! Udora, really!''

"Don't pull such a face. They add the perfect touch if you'll just think about it. Sometimes these affairs tend to become a bit gamey, if you know what I mean.'' She pinched her nose. "The crowds and the crush...''

"Conscience tells me we would be wise to postpone this party.''

"Pistachions! You know it would be impossible. Besides, it will be *the* event of the Season.''

"If anyone stays long enough to sit down.''

"Oh, they shall. I chanced to meet Peter Treadway at the coffee shop where I stopped to rest my feet. He's promised to come, and bring his flute.''

"Truly? I must admit, I'm impressed.''

"And I warrant he'll bring his friends. I hope you have enough food."

"We shan't, if you continue to invite people."

Udora cast a curious look. "Has Lord Bancroft been round to call this afternoon?"

"No. And since he was quite furious at me for having removed his precious name-plate, I doubt that he will put in an appearance."

"Nothing could keep him away." Udora dimpled. "Unless it would be that ogre of a mother. But then I doubt he keeps her informed of his every movement. Take my word for it: he will be here."

"We shall see," Yvette said, all the while hoping that his anger had abated. It was foolish, of course, and ill-advised, but try as she might, she could not banish him from her thoughts.

PREPARATIONS FOR THE PARTY were going well early the next afternoon when the Carstairs came to call. Lady Emily blushed prettily when Yvette welcomed her and Lord Berrington into the library. It was all Yvette could do to keep from excusing herself to attend to her duties. She had been a domestic for too long to slip easily into the role of hostess in the presence of her former employers.

Lady Emily patted her swollen stomach and sighed. "Do forgive us for intruding, Yvette, Lady Udora. I know how busy you are, but James and I couldn't resist stopping in."

Lord Berrington settled onto the settee next to Lady Emily. "We received a letter from Lady Margaret and Mr. Harrington, who are presently in Scotland to buy woolens. They wanted us to extend their best regards."

Lady Udora arranged her skirts in a chair across from them. "I heard that they expect to return before your babe is due, Lady Emily. A pity they had to miss our party."

Lord Berrington adjusted his neckcloth. "Yes, indeed. Rumour has it that you are planning quite an unusual soirée."

Yvette blanched. "Truly? I had no idea that word had got outside the house."

"The servant grapevine, don't you know." Lady Emily leaned forward, her eyes sparkling. "Do tell me about it. I want so much to attend, but in my present condition I would create quite a scandal."

Yvette expelled her breath. "It would pale when compared to the scandal we are about to create."

"Indeed? How delicious. Tell me everything."

Udora, her red curls bouncing, clasped her hands together with obvious anticipation. "Why don't we just show them, Yvette?"

Yvette demurred, but her reluctance was overridden and she was forced to lead the way to the drawing room. Later, thanks to her frayed nerves, the only comment she could remember was when Lord Berrington took one look, whistled softly and said, "Open Sesame."

Both Lord Berrington and Lady Emily agreed that the room would surely cause a stir among the ton. Lady Emily expressed her opinion that curiosity would hold sway over the urge to snub an outsider for daring to step unbidden into the London Season.

Before they took their departure, Lord Berrington sent a generous supply of wine and a wheel of cheese round to the kitchen door. Lady Emily extracted a promise that as soon as the party was over the two women must come to call with a complete description of everything that took place at the party.

THE LATE AFTERNOON SHOWERS boded ill for the party's success, but as Udora had predicted, the sky cleared, leav-

ing the air clean and crisp. That evening Yvette heard the
first carriage approach the circular driveway a good fif-
teen minutes before the appointed hour. Maggie popped
her head in the doorway of the dressing room.

"'Er ladyship says I'm to do yer hair, miss. Will you be
ready soon?"

"Thank you, Maggie. I'm quite used to arranging my
own hair. You may tell Lady Udora that I'll be down directly." Yvette stood and smoothed the narrow panels of
the peach silk dress she had selected to wear. It was a trifle
opulent for her taste but the dress was one that had belonged to Lady Margaret and Yvette had added a third tier
to the graduated skirt to give it enough length. A quick
glance in the Empire mirror assured her that it looked quite
fetching. Udora had lent her a beaded shawl in the sheer-
est of sapphire blue silk to draw attention from Yvette's
hair, which Udora insisted was a mousy shade of black.

She was right of course, but it was the best that could be
done with it, given the present circumstances.

By the time Yvette arrived downstairs, Udora was already mingling with the guests. Her saffron silk dress
looked as if it might have come from one of Ali Baba's
dancers. Yvette nearly gasped when she saw that the hem
had been gathered round Udora's ankles and tiny bells
were attached to the toes of her gold satin slippers.

The next few hours were half nightmare, half euphoria.
Word of the party had spread quickly across London.
Those guests fortunate enough to arrive early reclined on
the huge pillows while they drank arrack punch and dipped
sippets of cake into the sweet liquor. Others stood in
groups around tables laden with dried fruits, nuts, pastries and dainty sweetmeats. Guests who chose to arrive
fashionably late were dismayed to find the lane congested
with carriages of every size and shape, forcing the drivers

to jockey for position even before they managed to discharge their passengers at the main entrance.

The guests held one thing in common: after their initial shock wore off, nearly everyone entered into the spirit of the party, a fact that contributed to an unusual sense of camaraderie among the normally staid revellers.

Yvette made an effort to circulate among the various groups. Once the subject of the room's decor was out of the way, conversations ranged from the latest bout of Gentleman Jackson at his Bond Street gymnasium, to Kean's electrifying performances at Drury Lane, to the friendly debate between Walter Scott and the publisher, John Murray, who were holding court at one end of the room, to the latest fashions smuggled out of Paris.

Udora popped a pastry into her mouth as she approached Yvette. "Be warned, my dear. I let it slip that the pastries came from a cherished but secret French patisserie. So much more impressive, don't you think, than saying they came from our own kitchen? Of course every hostess worth her salt is trying to pry the name of the establishment from me."

Yvette laughed. "I might have known you'd try that. It's unfortunate that I already admitted to having baked them myself."

"Disgusting! You are too honest for your own good. Have you seen Lord Bancroft?"

"No. You see, I was right." She tried to keep the disappointment from her voice. "He's crossed us off his list. I doubt that he'll come here again."

"Pistachions! He's probably simply lost in the crush." Udora fanned her cheeks. "Have you ever seen anything like it? Never in my wildest dreams would I have dared expect so many people to attend our salon. I've let it be known that we shall welcome visitors each Thursday for informal gatherings.''

"Every Thursday?'' Yvette gasped, but before she had a chance to give Udora a proper set-down, someone else had demanded her attention.

"Mademoiselle Cordé, you must honour us with a song,'' the bandy-legged man said in a rather loud voice. His request was echoed by a dozen people until Yvette had to protest.

"I would be pleased to do so, but as you see, I have no piano.'' A murmur of disappointment arose in the immediate vicinity. "Instead, perhaps I can prevail upon Mr. Treadway to play a few more encores on his flute,'' Yvette said, casting her gaze upon the respected musician. He readily agreed and room was made for him beneath one of the main chandeliers.

"For shame. You have disappointed them, mademoiselle,'' a deep masculine voice murmured in her ear.

"I'm sorry, I . . . Oh, 'tis you, Lord Bancroft. I might have known.''

"Did you think I wouldn't attend your party?''

"The thought never crossed my mind.''

He gave her a look that plainly chastised her for the blatant falsehood and took her firmly by the arm. "Come with me.''

"I will not,'' she said, but short of losing a limb, she had little choice in the matter. "Where are you taking me?''

"To the attic.''

"Really! You are most uncivil.''

He ignored her, and in fact did not say another word until they had climbed the narrow steps to the storage room under the eaves. "Be careful of your gown,'' he admonished. "There is dust everywhere.''

"I can see that. What is the purpose of this excursion? Is it your intention to remove the few relics you left behind when you stripped my house?"

He grinned. "If truth be told, I had forgotten all about the goods and furniture stored up here." His free hand swept the room. "Take it, take it all with my compliments, mademoiselle."

He released her arm and cautiously stepped over a pile of books to reach a cupboard from which he extracted a lute made of exquisitely inlaid woods. It was pear-shaped, with a vaulted back and a fretted neck. He tightened the tuning pegs and strummed the strings.

Yvette gave him a dry look. "I would thank you, my lord, but the goods are already mine by right of purchase." She looked at the musical instrument he held. "Is that what you dragged me all the way up here to see? It's lovely, I'll admit, but I hardly see the significance."

"Do you play?" he asked, slanting a look over at her.

Despite herself, the blood rushed to her face. "The only instrument I lay claim to is my voice."

"I guessed as much. Do you think you could sing accompanied by the lute?"

"What do you mean you guessed as much?"

"I meant no offense. You must admit that one in your unfortunate position might find it impossible to..." He paused.

Yvette laughed and decided to take pity on him. "You do have a way of digging yourself into a hole, Lord Bancroft. As to your question: yes, I suppose I could sing to a lute's accompaniment, though of course it would depend on the skill of the player."

"I'm pleased to hear you say so." He motioned to the stairway and bowed deeply. "After you, mademoiselle."

"Do you mean this is all we came up here to do?"

He laughed. "Did you think I had it in mind to ravish you, Yvette?"

"Guard your tongue, sir!" she said, moving quickly in front of him. The nerve of him, speaking so boldly, and using her given name so freely. He caught her arm and stopped her midway down the stairs.

"Thoughts of you are constantly in my mind, Yvette, and have been since the day I first saw you sing. I swear that you have bewitched me. Tonight, after everyone has left, I wish to speak to you again about an arrangement to suit both our conveniences."

Half turning, she lifted her head to meet his gaze. "You know my feelings on that subject. I beg you not to mention it again. I doubt, Lord Bancroft, that we shall ever become more than guarded friends, and indeed I wonder if we can ever cease being enemies."

His eyes smouldered. "I am not your enemy, but I promise this, mademoiselle, that one day soon we shall become much, much closer than friends."

Her heart nearly stopped at the intensity of his voice. Before she could properly set him down he kissed her softly on the mouth. He was the first to pull away, a fact he was quick to note, judging by the way his eyes glittered with triumph when she finally opened her eyes to confront him.

His voice caressed her. "There, you see, mademoiselle? It's just as I said."

She dragged her gaze away from him and lifted the hem of her skirt. "You are despicable, Lord Bancroft. A conniving, treacherous rakehell, and certainly not the gentleman you pretend to be."

"That does not signify. What matters is that I always get what I want and at the moment, I want you."

"'At the moment,'" she said, mimicking his tone. "Forgive me if I'm not flattered, my lord. I do not choose to be any man's *moment*."

The last few words were spoken over her retreating shoulder, but Andrew knew she was not as angry as she pretended to be. He suspected that she had come to enjoy these verbal sparring matches as much as he did. *Time,* he thought. Time will bring her round. Tucking the lute under his arm, he followed her down to the lower floor where she disappeared into the drawing room.

Lord Whitlow, a wineglass in one hand, a plate of pastry in the other, leaned indolently against the corridor wall. "What ho, Andrew. Have you been sneaking kisses in the attic with our raven-haired lark? Perhaps I placed my wager on the wrong side."

"Mind your tongue, Percy," Andrew cautioned the corpulent blond-haired man. "And kindly save your deviltry for White's. I was a fool to agree to the bet in the first place."

"Afraid of losing your favourite mount? You still have nearly a month to unlock the lady's golden charms." He wiped his hand across his mouth. "Greebers doesn't have a chance of besting you from the way it looks to me. You practically have his prize phaeton parked in your stable."

Andrew paled. The wager that had begun as a prank, a way of passing another boring evening at the club, had become more like a noose about his neck. Neither losing his favourite horse nor winning the carriage from Greebers meant anything to him now that he had got to know Yvette. She fascinated him more than any woman had ever done. He wanted her, yet he wanted to protect her.

But her temper was something to be reckoned with. If she ever found out about the wager, she would stop at nothing to avenge herself. Without acknowledging Whitlow's compliment, Andrew strode into the crowded drawing room.

He was grateful when the crowd closed around him and his thoughts were diverted from the wager. Andrew lifted the lute and strummed a few notes of an old melody before readjusting a tuning peg.

"Play something, Lord Bancroft," a woman cooed from the edge of the crowd.

"Yes, do. Something lively, my lord. 'Donkey and the Pig,' or 'Foxes in the Meadow,'" another voice echoed.

Andrew strummed a few lines then spoke softly. "Perhaps Mademoiselle Cordé would consent to sing?" He smiled, knowing that she would refuse him if he were to ask, but she would never refuse her guests. A moment later she was brought to his side, her eyes mutinous.

"It seems I've been summoned to sing. What would you play, Lord Bancroft?"

He looked bemused. "This one? 'The Master and the Maid.' I'm sure you know it." His fingers skipped along the strings, plucking out a familiar melody.

Yvette felt her face turning red. "I'm afraid I don't know that song, Lord Bancroft."

"Of course you do. I heard you singing it not three days ago. It begins like this:

"One April day on a garden stair
A nobleman met a maid so fair."

Yvette knew the song about the innocent maiden who met the nobleman and was so entranced that she became his willing slave. She also knew that Lord Bancroft had chosen the song simply to embarrass her.

She fixed him with a smile which failed to reach her eyes. "Yes, I remember. Afterwards, perhaps we might try the ballad about the country miss who jilted the proud lord in favour of the handsome shepherd. 'Home to the Glen,' I believe it's called."

He touched two fingers to his forehead in mock salute, then moved over to make room beside him on the narrow bench.

She unclasped her fan and drew it across her palm. "Thank you. I prefer to stand."

He nodded and ran his fingers over the lute strings. Yvette took up the melody after the short introduction and her voice rose sweetly as she became more confident.

He was an accomplished player, she had to admit. His enthusiasm made up for an occasional wrong note but the crowd loved him, loved the two of them together. Yvette enjoyed it too, so much so that she would have continued on into the late evening. But Udora cautioned her about giving away too much of herself when her livelihood depended upon the money people paid to hear her sing.

It was Udora's suggestion that the guests be invited to join in the singing. During a lull in the music, while Yvette and Lord Bancroft took refreshment, Lord Dandridge, a rakehell known for his uninhibited love of fun, climbed up on the bench and lifted his glass.

"Hark, everyone, while I propose a toast." He waited while the room quieted. It didn't take long, Yvette noted. Dandridge, in his brilliant blue coat and knee breeches, his blond curls brushing his shoulders, was as handsome as he was popular. The jewels he wore on his hands glittered in the flickering light of the scented candles.

"A toast to our beautiful hostess, Mademoiselle Yvette Cordé, who has given us an evening of pleasure unequalled this Season. In honour of her exquisite voice, I dub this house The Lark's Nest."

The crowd applauded until she stood and thanked him. But he was not finished. "And to her beautiful companion, Lady Udora Middlesworth, whose beauty and wit is once again a challenge—" he winked "—and mayhap an invitation...to every mother's son." Udora was apparently undismayed by the subtle cut, or at least decided to play it so, because she laughed and dropped a curtsy as Dandridge continued. "And, last, but not least, to Lord Bancroft. May he go down in history as White's biggest winner."

A hush fell over the room. Yvette saw that Lord Bancroft was plainly unsettled by the remark. His face turned dark red above his high starcher and he quickly gulped his wine. Then the tide of conversation rose once more and the incident appeared to be forgot.

The group singing proved to be so popular that it was long after midnight before the guests began to disperse. Andrew took it upon himself to stand alongside Yvette and Udora as they bade their guests good night.

Yvette was ruffled by his perseverance. When they were alone for a few minutes she took him aside. "While I appreciate the fact that your talent added a certain something to our party, Lord Bancroft, I don't wish to impose upon you to act as our host."

He rocked back on his heels. "It is no imposition, mademoiselle. I find it comes quite naturally here at Waverly Lodge."

"Haven't you heard, my lord? The house has been renamed? From now on it is to be called The Lark's Nest. Appropriate, don't you think? Especially so, when you consider how much I cherish the lark's nest you gave to me."

"The toast was made in jest. This is still Waverly Lodge and will ever remain so. Mark my words."

Yvette smiled sweetly. "Would you care to place a wager? I understand you have a penchant for placing bets." The look he gave her was reward enough for all he had put her through that night. Instinct told her that the bet at White's concerned her. And she wasn't about to let him win.

CHAPTER NINE

THE DAYS FLEW BY with stunning swiftness following that first Thursday night salon. If Mr. Cruikshank's outrageous cartoons printed in the *Times* depicted The Lark's Nest in rather lurid terms, they did no harm to Yvette's popularity. She was invited to sing at Melbourne House in Whitehall, clearly one of her most successful forays into London Society. Her reward was an Etruscan vase which would pay for the furniture she needed, as well as providing upkeep of the house for several weeks to come. And in the end, the Turkish motif had proved so popular that Yvette gave in to Udora's wish to keep it for a few months longer.

It was at that very elegant party at Melbourne House that a noticeable change came over Andrew's mother. Alicia Waverly, Lady Bancroft, actually smiled at Yvette while she was singing a French lullaby. The reason became clear a half hour later when Lady Bancroft, coming upon her in a bedroom set aside for the use of the ladies, let it be known that she wished Yvette to entertain at a party she planned to give.

She flashed her heavily jewelled hands as she spoke with more animation than Yvette had thought the woman capable of. "It's going to be a garden party, mademoiselle, to unveil the gazebo which Mr. Nash designed for us. Of course there will be a large gathering of only the most influential members of the ton. I regret that your friends and...former employers, have declined my invitation, since Lady Emily is *enceinte,* but I trust that you shall find someone to talk to."

Yvette smiled at the transparent set-down. "Making friends has never been difficult for me, Lady Bancroft. In point of fact, your son has already offered his services as an escort, should Lady Udora and I accept his invitation to go as your guests."

"It had not occurred to me to include Udora Middlesworth's name on my list."

"If not, then I must, with reluctance, refuse your invitation. Lady Udora is my dear friend as well as my companion. I'm sure you understand."

"I had no idea that you, in your...circumstances, required a chaperon. But yes, since you insist, I shall see to it that both of you are sent invitations. Now, about your fee."

Udora, who had been standing with a group of ladies at the far side of the room, hastened to Yvette's side. "I couldn't avoid overhearing your invitation, my lady. Surely you must know that Mademoiselle Cordé would not stoop so low as to charge a fee." She turned to Yvette. "Really, my dear. I consider this an insult above half. You must, of necessity, decline."

Yvette was at a loss for words. Lady Bancroft's face turned first red, then white. When the silence lengthened, Yvette became desperate until she recognized the twinkle in Udora's eyes, where most people would have seen only contempt.

"I...er...I'm sure her ladyship meant no harm, Lady Udora," Yvette said. "I consider it an honour to be asked to entertain her *other* guests."

"But your book is nearly filled. Only yesterday I was forced to refuse a request from Baron von Wilhousen because of conflicting engagements.'' Udora turned her most condescending smile on the viscountess. ''I'm sure Lady Bancroft will understand. My goodness, there are so many marvellous entertainers available today.''

The viscountess looked stricken. ''We both know there is no one who can be compared to Mademoiselle Cordé.'' By this time Lady Bancroft had removed her gloves and had wadded them into a ball. ''I do beg your forgiveness. If I have made a *faux pas*...''

Udora dimpled. ''Your apology is accepted, my lady. Now if you will excuse us, I believe your son is waiting for us in the ballroom.''

Before either Yvette or Lady Bancroft had a chance to respond, Udora dropped a curtsy and pointed Yvette in the direction of the door, then closed it behind them.

Yvette pulled away from Udora's grasp. ''Really, Udora, I am quite disappointed in you. I thought I made it quite obvious that I wanted to accept her invitation.''

''As what? A servant? A menial hired to entertain while her favoured guests dine on pheasant and imported wines? Don't be a complete airling. Trust me, she will come begging you to forgive her. No—'' Udora tapped her fan on Yvette's cheek ''—what she will do is send her son. Tomorrow, I think. And I warrant that the little memento she contributes to the cause will go a long way toward paying the final instalment on your house.''

YVETTE WAS LESS CONFIDENT than Udora but her ladyship was rarely wrong. She dressed carefully the following morning in the hope that Andrew would call unexpectedly, as was often his wont. Udora also took great pains with her appearance, but by early afternoon her confidence was dwindling.

"I was so sure that witch of a viscountess would send her son a-begging for you to sing for them. I'm sorry, Yvette, if I've bungled this for you."

"It's not your fault, Udora. Lady Bancroft detests me."

"She doesn't detest you. It's only your background she objects to, not to mention her son's obvious obsession with you. She is determined to keep the blood lines noble. You know that, Yvette, and you must be very careful," she said, laying her newspaper aside.

"If somehow you can negotiate a marriage offer from Andrew it will be nothing short of miraculous. Anything less would be . . . well, temporary, I assure you."

Yvette stared out the window. "I would never consent to anything less than marriage. As for that, it is the furthest thing from my mind. There are too many other concerns to worry me at the present."

Their conversation was interrupted by McMasters, who cleared his throat. "I beg your pardon, mademoiselle. Lord Bancroft has arrived at the front door along with a drayman."

Before he had time to say more, Yvette jumped up and grabbed a poker from the fireplace. "*Sacré bleu!* He's come to empty the attic. And after he told me the rest of it belonged to me!"

Lord Bancroft appeared in the doorway. A lock of his brown hair falling across his forehead gave him an endearing, boyish look, but his stance signalled his complete arrogance.

"I trust it is not your intention to use that poker, mademoiselle."

"You will be the first to learn differently if you attempt to remove another book, or vase, or piece of furniture from my house."

He smiled and spread his arms wide. "You wound me, mademoiselle. Do I have such thieving ways?" He was entranced by the way she bristled at him. Save for the brightness of her cheeks, which gave evidence of her temper, she looked winsomely demure in a sprigged muslin morning dress. "Tell her, Lady Udora. Tell her how she has misjudged my character."

Lady Udora came over and took the poker. "Look at the man, Yvette." She slanted a quizzical gaze from one to the other. "How can one doubt such innocence?"

"He's as innocent as Napoleon at Austerlitz," Yvette said. "What is it you want, Lord Bancroft?"

"Only a moment of your time. Would you come with me into the foyer?"

"I see no reason... Oh, very well."

He bowed and stood aside. "Lady Udora, perhaps you would care to join us?"

Her eyes twinkled. "The Royal Guards couldn't keep me away."

Yvette was the first to set foot in the entrance hall. Her way was blocked by a large monstrosity covered in a cotton sheet. "What is it now, Lord Bancroft? Have you brought a Trojan Horse?"

"See for yourself," he said as he whisked the covering aside.

"A piano!" Yvette cried. She rushed forward to run her fingers across the shining mahogany surface. "It's beautiful. But I don't understand. Why?"

"Why indeed?" His voice was husky. "A fine voice deserves a fine instrument. I know how difficult it is for you to rehearse for your concerts since you lost your piano."

"I didn't lose it, my lord. You took it."

"Be that as it may, it was old and out of tune."

"True." Yvette turned, meeting his warm gaze with her cold eye. "Of course the fact that your mother wants me to sing at her soirée has nothing to do with your sudden generosity."

Andrew looked genuinely dismayed, but Yvette knew how skilled he was at dissembling. It came as no surprise when he affected an innocent look and said, "The thought never occurred to me. Whether or not you choose to sing at my mother's party is entirely your decision. I trust, however, that it won't alter our friendship." He laughed. "Of course, your refusal would certainly lower me in my mother's estimation. She considers failure to be quite beneath me."

"I'm sure you do everything in your power not to disappoint her. You don't deny, then, that the viscountess has asked you to intervene on her behalf?"

He put his hand over hers. When she looked up to meet his gaze there was a challenge in his eyes that was echoed in his voice. "Of course she did, Yvette. But only this afternoon. The piano was purchased this morning. It is my gift to you."

Yvette was taken aback and quite unprepared to respond. Her voice was unsteady. "How very generous. I can't accept it, of course."

"The gift is free of any obligation on your part, if that is what concerns you."

Lady Udora stepped forward. "If you will forgive my intrusion, mademoiselle, it behoves me to suggest that you thank his lordship for his thoughtfulness and accept it in the manner in which it is given." She smiled bewitchingly. "I hope, Lord Bancroft, that you will not forgo the lute, now that we have a piano. Our guests were enthralled by your performance."

"You are too kind, Lady Udora."

Yvette pressed her hands together. "Please forgive me for jumping to conclusions, Lord Bancroft. It was unkind of me, particularly in the light of your generosity, but I cannot accept so expensive a gift. It would be unseemly."

"Nonsense. Lady Udora has already given her nod. Besides, I would take it as an affront to my good name. Please do me the honour of accepting this insignificant gift as a small token of my esteem." His eyes met hers and neither of them was willing to break the contact.

The moment seemed to last forever. It took all of her will-power to drag her attention away from that compelling gaze. She retrieved her hand and sat down at the bench. "If word gets out that the piano was a gift from you, we both shall be placed in a compromising position. However—" she raised an eyebrow "—if we let it be known, should questions arise, that the piano was intended to replace the furniture you removed, then the gossips would have nothing to chew on."

He frowned and seemed about to protest, but instead shrugged his shoulders. "If you insist. It shall be as you say." At the same time it occurred to him that Yvette somehow always managed to best him.

She ran her fingers across the smooth keys. "I only wish I had learned to play with more skill than I possess."

"That would be gilding the lily. There is always someone to play for you, but only your voice can do justice to the song. Where would you like the piano placed, mademoiselle?"

"In the salon. Between the east windows."

"A wise choice. I'll ask the drayman to take care of it before I leave," he said, signalling the butler for his beaver.

Udora dimpled. "Surely you aren't leaving so soon?"

"I've no wish to intrude."

"Nonsense. You are not intruding. Yvette and I were just about to have a cup of tea. You'll join us, of course."

Lord Bancroft appeared to hesitate, then looked at Yvette for confirmation.

"Please stay. I haven't thanked you properly nor adequately apologized for mistrusting your motives."

Andrew looked at her from beneath his shaggy eyebrows. "I beg of you not to apologize, for if you do, then I must confess that my motives are not always so pure as they are today."

Yvette's voice was cool. "We are well apprised of that fact, my lord." She stood and walked past him in the direction of the library. At the last minute she turned. "If it would soothe your relationship with your mother, then I would be pleased to sing at the unveiling of her new gazebo."

He clasped his hands together. "Superb! I assure you she will be overjoyed at the good news. It should prove to be a significant party. Some of the finest people in London Society have sent their acceptances."

"Yes. So your mother has led me to understand," Yvette said drily.

Udora pointed her toe and swished her skirt in a comic imitation of the minuet. "It's going to be the most exciting party of the year. I can feel it in my bones."

THE NEW PIANO proved to be a welcome addition to the Thursday night salons. That is not to say that Andrew was never asked to play the lute, for at least one duet between him and Yvette became *de rigueur* at each of her gatherings. It was on the occasion of the third salon that Lady Margaret, recently returned from the north country, where she and her husband were buying woolens for their establishment, took Yvette aside.

"Who would have thought, my dear, that you could accomplish so much in just a few short weeks? The house is lovely; the drawing room in particular," she said with a decided twinkle in her eyes. "You know what they're saying about you, don't you?"

Yvette smiled. "I've been afraid to read the newspapers since Cruikshank began drawing those horrendous cartoons of me. I know I shouldn't ask, but just what are they saying?"

"That you are the most exciting thing that has happened in London since the duchess ran off with her dance instructor."

"That's rather a mixed compliment, but not so offensive as I had expected. I was afraid..."

"But that isn't the top of it, Yvette. There is considerable speculation about you, where you came from, who your parents were, and just how and when you arrived in this country." Lady Margaret took a sip of fruit punch and made a face. "Nasty stuff, this, but I've given up the sherry since my marriage." She fixed her with an uncompromising gaze. "You're quite a mystery, you know. There are those who say you are the illegitimate daughter of the famous French singer, Massina."

Yvette tensed. "It simply isn't true, nor is it true that my father was the naval hero, Jean-Pierre Cordé."

"Indeed?"

The one-word question was an open invitation to clarify rumours, something Yvette was afraid to do. She was saved from answering when Lord Bancroft approached.

"Lady Margaret." He bowed. "It is a pleasure to see you looking so well. Mr. Harrington says that he has regained his youth since he had the good fortune to meet you at Countess Lieven's soirée."

"That husband of mine has kissed the blarney stone too many times. May I return the compliment, Lord Bancroft? Never have I seen you appear so handsome as when you and Yvette were entertaining us with your duet. You look well together."

"Thank you, my lady. I have been telling the mademoiselle much the same thing for weeks now."

Yvette shot a warning look at him and would have set him down, but was interrupted when McMasters came up to them and bowed.

"I beg your pardon. I have a message for her ladyship," he said, handing Lady Margaret a folded paper on a silver salver.

She took the note and lifted her quizzing glass to her eye. "Good news! It seems that Lady Emily has just given birth to a boy. I must go to her. McMasters, will you see that my carriage is brought to the entrance? Lord Bancroft, I wonder if you would seek out Mr. Harrington and tell him I wish to leave?"

"Of course, Lady Margaret. At once."

"That's a dear boy." She patted his hand. "I would be remiss in my manners if I failed to ask you to bring Yvette round in a day or two to see the new baby. I know the family counts you both high on their list of intimates."

Yvette would have been more comfortable going alone, but Andrew inclined his head. "I give you my word, Lady Margaret, that Yvette and I will come round as soon as her ladyship is receiving."

"Excellent. I'll leave word with Yvette when the time is right."

A few minutes later Mr. Harrington approached with his wife's cloak and Yvette and Andrew saw them to the front door. After they had gone Lord Coddington came up to Yvette.

"Mademoiselle Cordé," he said, sweeping an elegant bow. "I've been hoping for days for an opportunity to speak to you alone."

"Yes, Lord Coddington. I am at your disposal. Shall we sit down?"

Andrew surveyed the aging, but still handsome nobleman with suspicion. "Percival? Good to see you. How are those *four young girls* of yours getting on?" The undue emphasis was quite apparent.

Coddington frowned. "Quite well, thank you, Andrew."

Yvette saw that he was unsettled and she looked pointedly at Andrew. "Lord Bancroft, would you be a dear and see if the punch bowl needs refilling."

The errand was so transparent as to be ridiculous but Andrew got the message. "If you will excuse me?" He scowled and strode in the direction of the buffet table.

Yvette turned her attention to the tall, slightly balding man at her side. The widower was still near his prime. His sandy-brown hair was carefully brushed to lie flat against a well-shaped head. His grey knee-breeches and black waistcoat were of a fine material and cut that could only have been made by a skilled tailor. His cravat was held in place by a diamond-and-ruby stickpin.

Yvette smiled. "Now then, Lord Coddington..."

He looked nervous. "What I have to say, mademoiselle, is best said straight out."

"It sounds serious indeed." She made an effort to keep her tone light. Intuition warned her in advance of his intentions. "I think we can have a degree of privacy in the alcove, if you would care to join me."

She seated herself on a padded bench but he remained standing. It took several turns of conversation about his house in London, his country estate in Devon, his staff of servants, and at last, his four young daughters. The daughters had come as a surprise to Yvette. This wasn't the first tête-à-tête she had shared with the aging widower, but thanks to Andrew, it was the first time Percival Clinton, Marquess of Coddington, had mentioned his children. At last he came round to the reason for the private audience.

"*Harrumph*. You must know, Yvette, my dear, how much our little talks have come to mean to me. *Harrumph*. I daresay since you arrived on the social scene, I've thought of nothing else."

"I, too, have enjoyed our little talks, Lord Coddington, but I don't wish you to think that it means..."

"Please, just let me finish. Truth be told, I see too little of you, what with the crush of people. I want a significant friendship." He was alert enough to know that his suit was not going well and he held up his hands to forestall a refusal.

"*Harrumph*. I'm not asking you to compromise your good name, mademoiselle. All I ask is the right to court you with all due respect, with the intention that if you come to see me in a more favourable light, then I might one day soon request your hand in marriage."

Yvette was appalled. It wasn't what she had expected. She clutched the edge of the bench. "You do me great honour, Lord Coddington, and I thank you for your offer. Your friendship means a great deal to me." She struggled for the right words to soften the blow. "But I must, in all honesty, tell you that marriage is out of the question."

"Because of your birth? Truly, mademoiselle, it matters not one whit to me."

"I'm afraid it goes beyond that, my lord. Although I treasure our friendship, I am not in love with you."

"*Harrumph, harrumph.* Time could change that, Yvette."

She reached for his hand. "I'm sorry. I do hope that our friendship will continue."

He helped her to her feet and bowed. "I haven't given up, my dear. You would make a beautiful marchioness. I would be very good to you."

"I'm sorry, Lord Coddington, but now I must return to my guests." She touched his hand. "Please know that I am fond of you and no one, not even Lady Udora, shall know of this little exchange."

"Decent of you. *Harrumph.* But this will not be the end of it. I'm a determined and wealthy man, my dear. Anything you wanted would be handed to you on a gold platter."

She shook her head briefly. "If you will excuse me, I have guests to attend to."

But he wasn't so easily got rid of. For the rest of the evening, Lord Coddington was like a shadow at her side, never intruding, never speaking, but always there. It was only when Yvette sought the privacy of a bedroom that was set aside for the ladies that she was able to escape him.

Lady Strawbridge readjusted the emerald clip which held a sheer capelet round her shoulders. "I perceive, Mademoiselle Cordé, that you have made yet another conquest. Your third, I think, for the evening."

Yvette laughed. "You give me too much credit. Lord Billingsly was too far into his cups to know what he was doing, Lieutenant Sterling has been at sea so long that he would be attracted to anything without fins, and Lord Coddington spoke of his four little daughters."

"You have him on leading strings, of course," said Mrs. Hervey. "He can't see beyond your pretty face."

It was a well-known fact that Mrs. Hervey had set her cap for him ever since she had lost her title after her husband's sudden demise. She had bragged openly that the next time she wouldn't settle for a mere baronet, but would marry up, in accordance with her deserved station in life.

Yvette straightened the combs and brushes on the dressing table. "Lord Coddington is a dear, Mrs. Hervey, but we are simply good friends."

Lady Fullerton smoothed her black lace mantilla. "Don't be misled by Yvette's following, my dear. We all know that it is Lord Bancroft who is dancing attendance upon Mademoiselle Cordé. All she has to do is snap her fingers."

Mrs. Hervey laughed. "Not if his mama's still able to breathe."

Lady Fullerton lowered her voice to a conspiratorial level. "Tell us, Yvette. Is it true that Lady Bancroft has asked you to sing at her garden party?"

"How did you hear that bit of gossip, Amelia?"

"It was my abigail. She heard it from my upstairs maid who heard it from Cook. She is aunt, I believe, to the Bancroft driver, who heard this choice morsel from their butler."

"Are you denying it?" Lady Strawbridge demanded. Her eyes sparkled with anticipation. "We've all been dying to know if Alicia will fall from her top-lofty position long enough to ask you to entertain."

They waited breathlessly for Yvette's response, but she smiled and put her hand to her ear. "Oh, dear. If you will excuse me, I do believe that someone is calling me."

Mrs. Hervey snorted. "No doubt it's Coddington." She said something else but Yvette had already closed the door. Only their laughter followed her into the hallway.

Lord Bancroft caught her arm the minute she came into the corridor. "Where have you been hiding for the last ten minutes? Everyone has been looking for you."

"Why? Is anything wrong?"

"Nothing is ever right when you are out of sight." The dark tone in his voice brought her up short.

"What is it, Lord Bancroft? What has happened?"

"Nothing, yet. I want to know what Coddington wanted to say to you that required such privacy."

"It was nothing, really. Lord Coddington merely wished to tell me how much he enjoyed the party."

"Indeed? Then why is he going round looking like the pig who fell into the vat of sherry?"

"I have no idea."

"Look at him. He's never been this high in the trees. He's drawing an audience."

"So it seems."

A trill of excitement seemed to pass over the room like an ocean tide on the rise. Lord Coddington was helped up to a raised platform where he stood for a moment then clapped his hands. "Your attention, please, my lords, my ladies, friends. I have news to bring to you."

The room fell silent. He waited as if forming his words in his head. Whether or not it was intended, the pause heightened the drama to an excruciating degree.

Lord Coddington straightened to his full height and clicked his heels. "It is my pleasure to tell you that I have just offered for the hand in marriage of Mademoiselle Yvette Cordé."

A roar rose up round the room. It was equalled only by the roar in Yvette's head. He wouldn't! He couldn't! But he had.

Andrew looked down at her. His eyes seared her face as she stood open-mouthed. It was with difficulty that she managed to speak.

"It's not as you think, Andrew."

He swore an oath too dark for a lady's ears, and stormed from the room.

CHAPTER TEN

YVETTE STARTED to follow him, but she was immediately engulfed in a circle of well-wishers. It was impossible to hear what everyone said, but she knew from the expressions on their faces that they were shocked by the announcement of her sudden betrothal.

When the clamour subsided to a manageable noise, Lady Udora elbowed her way through the throng to Yvette's side. "Are you out of your mind? Can I not leave you alone for ten minutes without your making a fool of yourself?" she hissed in her ear.

Yvette was distraught and allowed Udora to pull her to one side. "Lord Coddington spoke out of hand. I made it very clear to him that I couldn't accept his proposal. Oh, Udora! What shall I do?"

"Do? The choice is yours, unless you care to leave it to Lord Coddington to be the arbiter. Considering only social standing and financial security, you could do worse than landing a marquess. But if he isn't your cup of tea, then you must certainly clarify matters before the night is out. It would be disastrous if word gets about that you have accepted his proposal." She fanned herself in agitation. "Great pistachions! Where is Lord Bancroft? If he gets wind of this..."

"He already has. He left the moment Coddington spoke out."

"Men! Well, never fret. We shall get through this yet. The first thing you must do is to stand up there and tell everyone the story was cut from whole cloth."

"I cannot do that. It was, of course, but it would destroy Coddington's honour. I couldn't bring myself to make him the laughing-stock of London."

"It would serve him right, the old goat. Then do think of something, and whatever you do, don't let anyone suspect you're browsick."

Udora turned and smiled bewitchingly as she clutched the sleeve of a young man in an elegantly cut wine-velvet coat. "Charles, my sweet. Would you clear the way for us? Mademoiselle is going to speak."

By the time they reached the platform Yvette's stomach was a-flutter. Good wishes rained upon her from all sides, but somewhere along the way, the power of speech had deserted her. It was then that Udora took the ribbons. She raised her hands for silence. Relief washed over Yvette when she realized that Udora was going to take charge of the whole situation.

"My good friends, may we beg your silence?" Udora said, then stopped as she looked uncertain of how to proceed. She spoke from behind her hand. "Either you think of something quickly or I'll tell them he lied."

Yvette was stunned. "You can't. He would be devastated." She stepped forward and waited again for the noise to cease. "It seems," she said, her voice quivering, "that there are those among you who find nothing more exciting than giving and accepting a challenge. Such was the case tonight. I am flattered by the attention, but dear friend that he is, Lord Coddington would be the first to admit than an agreement between the two of us would be untimely. Of course not one of you believed him for an instant."

The crowd murmured and a few titters were heard in the background; then Yvette continued. "It took a brave man to accept the challenge of a certain misguided soul, who shall remain nameless. In announcing our supposed betrothal, Lord Coddington has won the bet. Not only that, he has indicated that the two hundred guineas he has won shall be donated to the Society for Orphans and Foundlings. I'm sure his generosity deserves praise."

There was stunned silence for an instant. Then someone at the back of the room began to laugh. It signalled that Yvette's story was accepted, if not believed, and the room exploded with applause. Lord Coddington, who had been standing off to one side of the room, smiled tightly and bowed. When Udora took it upon herself to announce that another round of wine would be forthcoming, the party resumed with everyone in high good humour.

Mrs. Hervey was especially pleased. She beamed her relief. "I must confess, Mademoiselle Cordé, that I truly believed that Lord Coddington had offered for you."

"What utter nonsense," Yvette said. "But he is a very lonely man. If you were to give him a little encouragement, a little hint of your feelings—" she looked meaningfully at her guest "—who knows what might happen?"

"Oh, surely you are teasing me. No?" She fluffed her hair and chewed her lips to bring up the colour. "Well, we shall see, shan't we? I think I just might recall how to flirt if I made a tiny effort," she said, moving in Coddington's direction.

Udora groaned. "You've just thrown away the keys to a fortune. But never fear, *ma chérie*. He was too old for you anyway. 'Tis far better to train them yourself than to take on another woman's mistakes."

"And I thought it was you who told me that a man advanced in years was the better prospect, since he was too old to chase the cat and only a step or two from his eternal rest." Yvette chuckled.

Udora sniffed. "You've doubtless mistaken me for someone else, though I suppose there are those women who see marriage as a necessary step towards widowhood. But trust me, Yvette, you are far too young to abandon the more intimate joys of marriage."

Yvette blushed, not only at what Udora had said, but at the mental image of Andrew that suddenly sprang into her thoughts. Andrew and his broad shoulders and deeply smouldering eyes. Where was he now?

YVETTE SOMEHOW MANAGED to survive the evening, but the following days proved far more difficult. Gossip had it that Andrew, Lord Bancroft, had taken his prized bay that same night and ridden alone to the north country. The Lark's Nest seemed empty without his entertaining, if not always charming, company. Truth be told, she missed his forthrightness and his daggerlike wit. But her real concern was that he had left too abruptly to learn the truth about Coddington's untimely attempt to force Yvette into a betrothal.

She was too out of sorts to accompany Udora and her young friend, Charles Willingsly, as they visited the shops or the art gallery or the lending library. Instead, she explored the boxes of books that were stored in the attic. One leather-bound tome appeared to be an old diary which was darkened with age and close to falling apart. It occurred to her that it ought to be returned to the Waverly family archives. She took it, along with a box containing assorted papers and books, downstairs to her room for future consideration.

The saving grace of those seven days without Andrew was the time Yvette spent at Berrington House. The baby, James, was the pride of the Carstairs household. Even Fredricks set aside his pompousness long enough to hold the baby for a brief time while the nanny went to fetch a blanket. When he, red-faced, passed the baby over to Yvette, she was filled with an indescribable sense of wonder that made her heart ache. She held the child to her breast and knew for the first time in her life that she must somehow contrive to have a family of her own.

She spoke of it to Udora later that night in her sitting room. Udora had just returned from seeing a play at Drury Lane. The honourable Charles Willingsly, second son of Lord Didderige, and a good seven years Udora's junior, had become something of a fixture at The Lark's Nest during the past two weeks. He was sweet, if rather shy. "Just the kind of lad I can train to my own style," Udora said, with a mischievous twinkle in her eyes.

"Will something come of it, do you think, Udora?"

She laughed. "I haven't decided. His mother, of course, will come down with a permanent megrim. His father, however, will have the good sense to recognize and appreciate my considerable connections, so I see no insurmountable difficulties there. Whether or not I settle on him depends on how well the dear boy wears in the next few weeks."

Yvette giggled. "You are entirely without conscience. You've had four marriages, Udora. Don't you ever regret not having had a daughter or a son?" she asked.

"I can't say that I do, but I'm young enough, should I change my mind." She wrinkled her pert nose. "They're messy little things, you know. Forever mewling and puking over everyone and everything. Just the time they become fit to live with they up and marry some little peabrain who doesn't know one end of the candle from the other. Blessed nuisance.'' She swivelled round to face Yvette.

''I perceive from those wistful cow eyes you're making that you've been to Lord Berrington's and have been seized by the maternal urge.''

Yvette flushed. ''I suppose I have.''

''Pity.'' She slanted a wide-eyed innocent look across at Yvette. ''If you'd played your cards right with Coddington you could have had four daughters ready-made. And not one of them in the bawling stage.''

Yvette laughed. ''I never know when to take you seriously, Udora. You're such a tease.''

She shrugged. ''Call it what you will if it makes you smile. It's been dreadfully long since Andrew left for the country. There is still no word from him, I presume?''

''None. I think we had better order up our own carriage for the party at Lady Bancroft's house tomorrow night. We can't expect him to come for us.''

''That is his loss. With the cream of London Society there, perhaps you'll find a man to put Lord Bancroft in his proper place.''

''Another man is the last thing I want. What concerns me is how I'm going to meet my final payment on the house.''

''The two could balance each other out, you know, providing the man is heavy enough in the purse.''

''If that were all that mattered, I could have done well with Lord Coddington. I still have time. Somehow I'll get the money.''

''My offer stands, Yvette. I'm willing to sponsor a loan.''

''No. I must do this on my own. Otherwise the house will never truly belong to me.''

"Don't fret," Udora said, going to the armoire. "Lady Bancroft's party should pay for a good portion of your debt.

"I see that Maggie has finished sewing the seed pearls on your dress. Without doubt it's the most attractive ballgown I've seen since before the war." She spread the pale-blue French silk over her arm. "Marvellous! It's time you wore something besides those cast-offs from Lady Margaret, attractive as they are. If this doesn't get Andrew's attention, nothing will."

"Yes, if he's even there. I heard a rumour that he had decided to return to the Indies."

"Don't believe it. I've seen the look in his eyes when he watches you. He wouldn't leave England without first seeking you out."

"I would like to believe it, though I know I am being foolish. Nevertheless, you give me hope."

THE FOLLOWING NIGHT, when they arrived at Bancroft House, Yvette doubted that Andrew would ever see the dress. As she predicted, he had not arrived with his carriage to take them to the party. True, he had not promised to do so, but it had been his habit in the past to see to their transport. Yvette sighed as she greeted her hostess.

"Is anything wrong, Mademoiselle Cordé?" Lady Bancroft asked in her smooth, oily voice.

Yvette forced a smile. "I'm quite well, thank you, your ladyship. May I compliment you on your lovely house. What a splendid collection of Persian carpets."

"They have been in the family for years. I'm sure Andrew has told you that we can trace our family back through many generations."

"We never speak of such things, but everyone is aware of your connections to the Royal family."

Lady Bancroft smiled radiantly. "Remote, of course, but nevertheless authentic." She looked down the end of her nose and adjusted her quizzing glass. "I perceive your accompanist has found his way to the piano. It has been placed inside our new gazebo. A John Nash design, don't you know. I thought perhaps you could sing the first two songs directly after the unveiling and the final two songs following the dancing in the garden. After that you and Lady Udora need not feel obligated to stay on. I know how exhausting it must be for you."

Udora, her patience ground to a powder, tossed the end of an ostrich feather boa over her shoulder. "You are without a doubt the kindest hostess on earth, Lady Bancroft. I've never known anyone, including the Duchess of Heatherwood, who is famous for her good manners, to go so far as to tell a guest when it is appropriate to leave."

Lady Bancroft started to smile, then recognized the ambiguous nature of the compliment. Her eyes hardened. "You do have a penchant for misunderstanding my intentions, Lady Udora."

"Do I indeed? May I say, in all candour, that you make your intentions remarkably transparent."

Yvette chose to interrupt before the ladies expressed themselves with even more honesty. "If you will excuse us, Lady Bancroft, I would like to make certain that my pianist has found the exact location of the piano."

The viscountess inclined her head in dismissal and Yvette led Udora towards the glass doors that overlooked the verandah and garden. Udora was fuming. "That woman is impossible. I wonder if she rides side-saddle on her broomstick."

Yvette curbed a burst of laughter. "I was dying to ask her if Andrew had returned, but I did not wish to give her the satisfaction."

"A wise decision. But I know how we can find out."

Yvette brightened. "How? Tell me at once."

"Just a moment." Udora went to a writing stand and withdrew a piece of foolscap. Taking the pen from the inkstand she wrote a quick message and folded the paper in half. Then, signalling to a footman, Udora gave him the note.

"Will you see that this is delivered to Lord Bancroft at once? It is an urgent message, to be given *only* to his lordship."

He bowed and clicked his heels. "At once, madam."

Yvette watched his retreating back as he climbed the wide, curved stairway to the next floor. She turned to Udora with considerable awe.

"Clever woman! What did you write in the note to Andrew?"

"That there was an urgent message for him."

Yvette drew a deep breath and expelled it slowly. "Oh, Udora! Whatever shall you say if he happens to come looking for you?"

Udora waved airily. "Not a blessed thing, my pet. Besides, he won't come looking for *me*. I signed your name."

"You what! You wouldn't! Please tell me you didn't." Yvette clutched at her.

"I most certainly did. Stop being such a ninnyhammer. If you want the man you must learn to fight like a man. With double-dealing deceit!"

Yvette lifted her gaze heavenwards. "Someone should have warned me about you. I thought you were supposed to keep me out of trouble, not send me rushing headlong into it."

"Pistachions! A little trouble never hurt anyone. Now, stop frowning. You're beginning to attract curious glances."

Within a few minutes they were swept into the main flow of the party. More than a few curious people questioned Yvette about the Coddington incident of the previous Thursday night. One bewhiskered little man was particularly persistent.

He stroked his rust-coloured beard. "Mademoiselle, pray tell us the name of the man who lost the dare," the Marquess of Doylestun begged. "I have the perfect challenge for him."

Yvette tapped his arm with her fan. "Now Rumford, you know I never break my promises. I couldn't possibly reveal her name, my lord."

"Egad! You said *her*. You don't mean to say 'twas a gel who bested old Coddington?"

"No. I don't mean to say anything." She laughed and dropped a mock curtsy before taking Udora's arm and moving away. The Marquess was heard to say, "That feisty bit of frippery is going to lead some young buck a merry chase."

Yvette's gaze quickly scanned the room. "Have you seen him, Udora?"

"No, if you're referring to Lord Bancroft. Nor have I seen that footman. Odd that he wouldn't have returned the note."

"All the footmen look the same to me in their gold and blue livery."

"Be serious, Yvette. They don't even remotely resemble each other. There is one with dark hair and long sideburns, a bit portly for my taste. Then I recall a little squab of a man who served our first glass of punch, and a blond man with beautiful thick hair but a decided tic in his right cheek. Our messenger was more foppish than the others, closely shaved with a bit too much pomade in his hair. Left him fusty-smelling enough to make one sneeze. Now my

Charles, dear man that he is, doesn't find it necessary to affect such frivolities."

"Really, Udora. You're making this up simply to entertain me."

"What utter rubbish. Oh look, here's our footman now."

He had seen them over the heads of the crowd and slowly made his way towards the two women. He bowed. "Madam, I regret that I was unable to deliver this message," he said, handing it back to Udora.

"Indeed? Does that mean that Lord Bancroft has not yet returned? Just when do you expect him to arrive?"

"I really couldn't say, madam. Is there something else?"

"No. Thank you." She turned to Yvette. "You see what I mean?"

"That Andrew has not yet returned."

Udora tapped her trim foot. "That would appear obvious. I was, however, referring to the footman. Fusty." She wrinkled her nose. "A pity, too. He's otherwise quite presentable."

The two women were accosted by a number of friends and acquaintances before they could make their way to the garden. The gazebo was still shrouded in a sheet of purple satin, waiting for the grand unveiling. The soft strains of music from a string ensemble drifting from beneath the cover gave evidence that the festivities were about to begin. Yvette left Udora's side just long enough to duck beneath the cover and assure herself that Mr. Armbruster was at his post in front of the piano. She advised him that she would be standing in readiness just outside the enclosure.

She didn't have long to wait. Within moments, footmen began shepherding everyone into the garden.

A large open area was bordered by shoulder-high yew hedges interspersed with marble statuary. Tall, gleaming columns held torches, whose flames danced light and shadow across the enclosure, where nearly three hundred people stood or were seated on marble benches. The satin-covered gazebo sat at one end of the oval.

Lady Bancroft, resplendent in lavender satin, wore her hair wound in a coronet round her head. It was decked with a myriad of sparkling diamond chips which winked as she moved. She was attended by four young men dressed in purple doublets and hose and wearing Phrygian caps on their heads.

Yvette looked over at Udora. "If you say one word I shall gladly strangle you."

Udora looked wide-eyed. "I don't know what you mean. I was simply admiring the rose-bushes."

The noise of the crowd quieted. At a blare of trumpets a dozen footmen pulled with one accord on the gold ropes that secured the gazebo's shroud and it fell away with a silken *whoosh*. A sigh of pleasure arose as the sparkling white structure sprang into view.

It was unusually lovely, Yvette admitted. The foundation was of a white stone embedded with a substance which sparkled in the light. The pillared framework was classic in its simplicity and was crowned with a Corinthian roof which extended out over the sides of the base. The interior of the gazebo was large enough to seat fifty people with ease.

The trumpeters lowered their horns and moved back as Lady Bancroft stepped forward to deliver her welcoming speech. Blessedly, it lasted only a few minutes and then she introduced Yvette who was handed into the gazebo and up the remaining steps to the platform. Mr. Armbruster looking totally at his ease, was well turned out in his black waistcoat and white starcher as he nodded that he was about to begin the introduction to the song.

Yvette took a deep breath. She smiled as she looked out over the gathering, and then her breath caught. Andrew was there. He was off to the side, leaning against a marble statue of Mercury. He neither moved nor gave any indication that he knew she had seen him, but he was aware of her. Yvette knew that he was very much aware of her.

Andrew felt a sharp wrench in his midsection and his mouth suddenly went dry. He hadn't expected seeing her again to affect him in this way. She stood so willowy and graceful in her gown of the softest blue, one hand resting lightly on the piano. It occurred to him that she looked more regal, more assured than ever.

A week in the country should have served to quench the fires that burned within him but they flared to life the moment he saw her. *God's blood!* He was a match to her torch, a moth to her candle, a flower to her Spring rain. He ached to hold her forever in his arms. Silently he cursed the noble blood that ran through his veins. He owed a duty to his family and he must not shirk that duty.

Her songs were melancholy tonight. No romping lambs on the meadow green, no elfin babes, no milkmaids dancing; only the plaintive cry of the nightingale and the songs of lost lovers wandering eternally in the darkened woods.

Yvette had somehow changed while he was gone. What had brought that haunted look to her eyes? Her music seemed to lay bare a secret core of sadness which burned deep within him. *Perhaps within everyone,* he thought as he looked at the people around him and saw the intensity of their response.

When she had finished her second song the listeners were too caught up in their emotions to respond immediately.

When at last they began to applaud, it was as if they were unable to let go of the moment.

Andrew recognized the emotion all too well. He had lived with it for a week. For her own sake Yvette must not be allowed to leave them in such a state of melancholy. He straightened and stepped up onto a small ledge at the base of the statue.

"Mademoiselle, would you be so kind as to sing 'A Jolly Good Ship and a Stormy Sea'?"

Their gaze met over the heads of the crowd. Yvette hesitated for an instant, then nodded. The crowd sighed its approval and then applauded. It was several seconds before she could begin the rollicking sea-shanty.

When her song and the inevitable encore were over, Yvette realized that Andrew had rescued her from a serious miscalculation. Her sad songs, born out of her own melancholy, had seriously affected the mood of the party. Lady Bancroft would never have forgiven her if everyone had gone home weeping. It was a lesson she would remember. Never again would she allow her own feelings to determine her choice of music.

Lady Bancroft touched her arm. "Splendid, mademoiselle. Now if you'll just stand by me for a few minutes while I make an announcement."

"Friends," she said, after her appearance on the platform had caught their attention. "I know how much we all enjoyed mademoiselle's little songs. At this time I would like to present her with a *small*—" she smiled to indicate that she meant quite the opposite "—token of my appreciation." She lifted a flat, rectangular object covered by a linen cloth. "This cherished painting by Bernard Chevalier has been in our family for many years. It is said that it was commissioned by my grandfather from Chevalier himself."

She whisked the cover off. "Yes. It's the very one we've kept hanging in the green drawing room for the last twenty-five years, but I can think of no one who might appreciate it more than Mademoiselle Cordé." She handed it over to her and Yvette looked at it carefully. Her eyes widened and her fingers tensed on the gilded frame but she managed to thank her hostess with an acceptable show of cordiality.

The crowd was obviously impressed by Lady Bancroft's unexpected generosity. Yvette saw the wide grin on Andrew's face and thought that he too looked unusually pleased.

Lady Udora took the painting from Yvette and passed it round so that those people standing nearby could better see it. When she was able to take Yvette aside, Udora's eyes were big and round.

"Did I not tell you Andrew's mother would be generous? The sale of this painting will surely pay the balance due on your house with a considerable sum to spare."

"*Mon Dieu!*" Yvette said. "I wish it were true. Unfortunately, the painting is a fake."

CHAPTER ELEVEN

"A FAKE!" Udora fumed. "Why, that conniving... But it can't be. How could you possibly know such a thing?"

"I know because the original was hung in my father's home in Lyons during most of the past twenty years." Yvette went pale and clasped her hand to her breast.

"Oh, come now, Yvette." Udora seemed more concerned with the revelation of the painting's value than of Yvette's past. "I don't understand how..." She shook her head. "Something isn't right here."

"Hush," Yvette cautioned recovering her composure a little. "No one must know. I regret having mentioned it."

"Pistachions! If this is true, we should tell everyone and let it be a lesson to her. Lady Bancroft has been sitting high in the saddle for too many years. It's time she had her comeuppance."

Yvette placed a firm hand on Udora's sleeve. "Just this once, please, *please* do as I say. I have no wish to embarrass Andrew's mother. We have nothing to gain by it, but we could lose everything. And smile!" she said as she saw Andrew coming towards them.

It was easier said than done. Udora was still too wide-eyed to do more than fan her flushed cheeks. Yvette was too numb to smile.

Andrew bowed, then took her aside into a tiny alcove where the roof-beams of the gazebo curved down to meet the pillars. "My compliments, mademoiselle. You have quite charmed my mother with your beautiful voice. You can't imagine how pleased she is, unless you could know, as I do, what great store she set in possessing the Chevalier painting.''

"If it has pleased your mother, then I feel that I have fulfilled my obligation." Yvette lowered her eyes then looked up to meet his troubled gaze. "Lord Bancroft, I can't thank you enough for requesting the sea-shanty. I found myself in a mood that was quite difficult to dispel."

He tugged at his waistcoat. "Since I have allowed myself the dubious privilege of self-pity for nearly a week, I know only too clearly how easy it is to fall into a dark mood. The sea-shanty lifted my spirits as well."

"I'm glad for that."

"But that wasn't all. The good news came to me just today that you are not, after all, betrothed to Lord Coddington."

"No. It was simply a misplaced pleasantry on his part. Lord Coddington was never a favourite of mine, though he has many good points. I think he hoped to take matters into his own hands and force me into a betrothal. But, as you see, the attempt failed."

"I should have known better. I was a fool to rush blindly off without hearing your side of it."

"Yes. You were," she agreed coolly.

He looked startled and then grinned. "And I have only myself to blame." He moved closer and rested his hand upon the pillar next to her head. "Where shall you hang the painting?"

Yvette looked away. "I don't know. I'll try to think of an appropriate place."

"Over the mantel in the library would be an excellent choice."

"I will consider it." She did not meet his gaze.

"I would like to call on you tomorrow, Yvette. Perhaps we might take a drive into the country. The meadows are greening and the streams are running full and swift."

"Udora isn't fond of the country. I could not go if she refused."

"I promise that she won't, for I'll invite young Charles Willingsly to join us."

Yvette laughed. "Yes, I think that might work. What do you know of him, Andrew?"

Only by a slight lifting of his eyebrow did he indicate that he noticed her use of his given name. That is, if one discounted his broad smile. He rocked back on his heels in a self-satisfied way. "What do I know about Willingsly? More than a little, I believe. Firstly, that he's feet over the fence-tops in love with Udora. He comes from good stock and though he enjoys a wager, no one could call him a high-flyer." He grasped the lapels of his waistcoat as he warmed to the subject. "I believe that Charles is the second son of a Lord Didderage—a Northern title. He's not likely to inherit the title, since his brother is a year or two older, but the lad's well provided for. He's young, twenty-five or so, and there's talk that he may follow his father into politics."

Yvette frowned. "A fact which should predispose the family to look with disfavour upon Udora."

"He has a mind of his own."

"Meaning that if he loves her enough he won't allow Society's dictates to keep them apart?" she challenged.

Andrew gave her a slow, speculative look. Too late he realized how that same judgement could apply to him. His voice was taut with words left unsaid. "Yes, mademoiselle. I suppose that is exactly what I meant."

She smiled, but it failed to reach her eyes. "I think perhaps we should be joining the others. It appears the orchestra would like to resume their place on the stand."

"Yvette. There is something you must understand."

"Indeed?"

"It is different for me. The title is already mine to uphold. I love you madly and would marry you in a moment if it weren't for the obligations of my heritage." His voice broke and he turned away from her to look out over the torchlit garden. "All my life I've been schooled in the necessity of my marrying appropriately. My family traces its heritage back to the Norman Conquest. Every viscount before me has been forced to put his own desires second to his concern for the family."

"I would never ask you to give up your heritage, Andrew. Neither would I offer my future children anything less than a loving and *complete* family."

His voice was ragged. He turned towards her and took her hands in his. "My dearest, don't you see what this is doing to us?"

Yvette silently blessed him for not laying the blame at her feet. "How could I not know? But it appears that neither of us has any choice in the matter." She backed away from him. "Please. Leave it for now. People are watching us."

"Tomorrow, then?"

She sighed. It was tempting to say yes, but she would only be courting heartbreak. She picked up her shawl and drew it protectively about her shoulders. "I'm sorry, Andrew. I must decline. Perhaps it would be prudent to keep some distance between us until we can think things through."

He paled visibly as he put his hands on her shoulders. "Don't draw away from me now, Yvette. I've been apart from you for too long."

She covered his hand with hers for one brief instant. "I fear it is something that each of us must learn to live with, *mon ami*."

"No. I can't let it go at that."

"You must. Excuse me, Andrew. I see Udora coming towards us."

He slowly released her. "May I have the honour of seeing you home? The painting may attract unwelcome attention, what with the riff-raff about the streets these days."

"Thank you. My driver is quite capable."

He bowed. "Until tomorrow."

"No, Andrew. I'll not be at home to you. I'm expecting guests."

"A minute ago you were only too willing to go with me to the country."

"I'm sorry. I had forgotten that the Carstairs plan to call."

"I can wait until they leave."

"No, Andrew. My butler will turn you away."

Udora came up to them before he had a chance to protest. He looked at each of the women, then turned and stalked away.

"What was that all about?" Udora asked. "I thought he was going to kiss you." She dimpled. "I wouldn't have frowned on a stolen kiss or two, but Lady Bancroft was spying on you with her lorgnette."

"It wasn't what you think, Udora. Please, let us not discuss it at the moment."

Udora patted her arm. "Of course. Come. I know of at least four gentlemen who would kill to add their names to your dance card."

Yvette expected to see no more of Andrew that night. Someone said that he had retired early, complaining of weariness after his long ride. She, too, would have chosen to return to the comfort of The Lark's Nest, but Charles and Udora were quite full of themselves and Yvette couldn't bring herself to separate them.

Later, when the dancing began in earnest, a door opened and a lone figure entered the small third floor balcony which overlooked the garden. Andrew hated his own weakness. He was drawn to Yvette despite his convictions, caught up in a current so strong that it swept everything else from his mind. Just knowing that she was in the same house was enough to drive away all thoughts of the sleep he so badly needed. He gripped the railing until his fingers ached. Seeing her passed from one man's arms to the next was like having salt rubbed into wounds already too raw to heal, and he swore in frustration.

Yvette caught a glimpse of him as she was whirled about the wooden dance floor that covered part of the lawn. She didn't lack for partners, but for all their differences they were all the same. If she tried hard she could pretend it was Andrew who held her in his arms, Andrew who dipped and bowed and pointed his toe, Andrew who twirled her round and round in an elaborate minuet.

But when she looked again he was gone. And for her, the evening was over.

It was some time before the dancing concluded and Yvette was able to perform her final two songs. She was then eager to depart, but was reluctant to suggest to Udora that she wanted to go home. Udora had charmed everyone with her warm wit and ready smile. Her smile fell most often upon Charles Willingsly, but Yvette noted with surprise that Lord Willingsly, Charles's father, had also succumbed to Udora's spell.

HOWEVER, WHEN SHE REACHED IT at last, The Lark's Nest felt singularly empty after the noise and crush of the party. Udora cheerfully collapsed on her bed, declaring that she was well on her way to finding an acceptable suitor. She sympathized with Yvette over her disappointment, but vowed that by morning she would see things in a different light.

"Now then," Udora said, sitting up and kicking her slippers across the room. "Tell me everything there is to tell about the painting." She propped a pillow against the headboard and leaned back. "But most of all, I want to know about *you*. It's time we put an end to the great mystery of Yvette Cordé."

Yvette looked at her for a moment, then turned and walked to the door. "There's nothing more that I can tell you than I have already said. I know the painting is a forgery because the original was hung in my father's house for many years." She kept her voice deliberately unemotional and steady.

"And what did your father do for a living?" Udora's curiosity was not to be denied."

"He . . . was a farmer."

"And where is he now?" Sympathy was warm in Udora's words.

Yvette's voice dropped to a whisper. "Dead. He was executed by one of Napoleon's generals."

"Oh my dear, and your mother?" Udora reached for her hand.

"Also dead. We fled to England to avoid capture. My mother became ill and died a few months later." Her unnaturally calm tone wavered at last.

Udora drew her into an embrace. "You poor girl! I am so sorry. I did not mean to awaken such sad memories."

Yvette shrugged. "It happened many years ago, but it is still very near to me. But, Udora, I do not wish to discuss it any more tonight."

"Of course. If there is anything I can do...?"

"There is nothing. Except just one thing. You must never discuss this with anyone. For reasons of my own I must keep my story a secret."

"But I don't see why..."

"Promise me, Udora." Yvette was implacable.

"Very well, I promise." Udora was clearly puzzled but gave in to her friend's insistence.

"Merci." Yvette said good-night then and went to her room. Apparently noticing the less than cheerful look on Yvette's face, Maggie turned down the bed, helped her undress, and left as quickly as possible.

Scarcely ten minutes had gone by when Yvette decided that sleep was impossible. Pulling a shawl around her shoulders, she relit the lamp and reached for the box of books and papers she had found earlier that day in the attic storeroom. She opened the musty-smelling box and discovered that it contained detailed drawings for her house, which had been in Andrew's family for so many years. Notes made in the margins seemed to have been made by Andrew's father.

Underneath the papers was the leather-bound journal whose pages had yellowed with age. She thumbed through it, wondering who had written it, but the first few pages were stuck together.

Going to her writing desk, she found the letter opener and carefully separated the aged leaves. There on the second page in carefully lettered script were the words, "This journal belongs to Archibald Wolgren."

"Mon Dieu," she said softly. "What is this?"

Archibald Wolgren. The name sent a chill through her veins, as events she had long tried to suppress came rushing back to her. Archibald Wolgren was the man her father had killed in a duel; the man whose brother-in-law vowed to find him and take revenge on him and his family until not one of them remained alive.

What was his journal doing here? She lay back against her pillows. Her respect for privacy made her momentarily rebel against reading another person's journal but, however unwilling, she was entwined in this man's life and perhaps her own fate was bound up in these yellowing pages.

Hours passed as she read and reread the journal, turning back to certain passages, puzzling over their meaning. One thing at least was now clear: Archibald Wolgren was Andrew's cousin through a remote connection. That explained why his personal effects had been stored in the attic. She had already known that it was Wolgren who had accused her father of embezzling money from his shipping firm. It was Wolgren who had challenged her father to a duel, a duel that resulted in Wolgren's death. And it was because of his death and the missing money that her father had been forced to leave England the same day or face arrest.

But the money had never been accounted for. Yvette knew enough of her father's character to know that he would never steal. Nor, indeed, did he need to. The family vineyard in Lyons, one of the most prosperous in France, was only one of his holdings. He had also been a part owner in the shipping company, in which Wolgren had owned a commanding interest.

Yvette's father had travelled widely to promote the sale of his excellent wines. It was on one such trip to London that he had met and married Yvette's mother. It was on another such trip that he had been wrongly accused of embezzling the shipping company's funds.

But the money. What happened to the money? She pressed her hands against her face. The question had haunted her ever since. She could not escape it. Somehow she must find the answer to the mystery, but to do so would surely endanger her own life. How many times in the past months had she thought she was being watched? No. She could not be too open about her intentions—or indeed her own identity.

There was little to be gained by telling everything, but there was much to lose: her livelihood, for one thing. Society might choose to snub her. And without her music she could not afford her newfound independence.

And now there was Andrew. If the truth of her past was made public, it would not take Andrew long to realize that Yvette was of noble birth. French, of course, but noble, nevertheless. The knowledge created a flood of warmth that dispelled the chill in her veins, but her sudden elation didn't last. For Andrew had already made his choice.

AT BREAKFAST the following morning Udora appeared disconcertingly cheerful in a pink-and-orange flowered morning dress that looked surprisingly fetching with her red hair. She collected her food from the sideboard and took a seat across from Yvette at the table.

"Now then, I demand that you tell me everything you left out last night. How does it happen that your family owned the original painting, and how do you know that it was the original and not a copy? I know how painful it must be to talk of it, but I think that is precisely what you need. You have kept everything to yourself too long."

"I shouldn't have said anything about the painting."

"Nonsense. If what you say is true, then it would surely have been an embarrassment had we tried to sell it. Truth will out, my dear, unfortunately." She smiled. "It would make life so much simpler if we could shade certain things a bit but it never truly pays. Now, tell me everything. I won't tell a soul."

Yvette would have laughed at that delicate attempt at dissembling, had she not looked so guileless. Instead, Yvette shook her head.

"It's nothing, really. It happens that my father was a close friend of the French painter, Bernard Chevalier. He lived in our town of Lyons where he used to come to our house for dinner. Then one day a patron of the arts chanced to see some of Chevalier's painting and agreed to sponsor him in Paris. Chevalier gave that painting of the canal to my father the day he left for Paris."

"I see. So it's true, then. The original couldn't have been hanging on Lord Bancroft's wall for all those years. What we have here is nothing but a copy."

"But a very good copy. I doubt that anyone would know it was not the original. Of course I would never attempt to pass it off as a genuine Chevalier."

"No, I suppose not. Have you thought, though, about what we're going to do to make the next payment on the house? You were counting on the money from this concert."

Yvette leaned her elbows on the table and rested her chin on her hands. "I've thought about little else. I have decided to sell the Chinese wedding chest in my sitting room to Lady Sedgeburry. It won't bring half its value but it will be a start and she has always coveted it. Perhaps Andrew would be willing to accept a partial payment until I can afford the rest.''

''Not likely. He's using the money as a weapon to get what he wants from you,'' Udora said tartly.

''Truly, Udora, I don't think he is. He said he would marry me if it weren't for his family obligations.''

''And you believed him?'' Her ladyship's eyebrows rose.

''Yes,'' Yvette said defiantly. ''The seven days he spent in the north have left him hagged-looking. Didn't you see it in his face?''

''Now that you mention it, yes, but I can't believe that Andrew would find it easy to break with tradition.''

''He said as much.''

''That's to be expected, but isn't he worth fighting for? You love him, Yvette. I can see it in your eyes and hear it in your voice when you speak his name. More to the point, he is as enraptured with you as you are with him. Is there no hope that you can change his mind?''

''I suppose I could manipulate him into marriage, but I don't want him on those terms. That is why I have decided not to allow him to call on me again.'' Yvette pushed her plate away.

''Oh, dear.'' Udora was strangely calm. ''Such drastic measures. But it's for the best, I suppose, under those circumstances.'' Udora buttered a scone. ''Well then, if your mind is made up, it's time you let yourself be courted by some of the eager young men who are less tied to their families' leading strings.''

Yvette gave her a dry look. She knew too much of Udora to accept that easy compliance. ''Please don't accept any engagements for me. I have far too much on my mind to be courted by anyone at present.''

"If I may say so, you do look a bit flaggy this morning."

"Then I had best do something about it," she said, rising from the table. "Lady Emily and Lady Margaret are stopping in to show us the baby, and a bit later, Lady Sedgeburry will be here to inspect the Chinese chest. After that, Mr. Armbruster and I have to plan my musical presentations for the party at Marlborough House next week."

Udora looked sceptical. "Don't think you've bamboozled me with all this talk of people to see and tasks to tend to. I think there's more that you've failed to tell me about your past. This might be just the time to have a serious talk."

Yvette pushed her chair up to the table. "Didn't you say that Charles is expected to call this afternoon? I seem to remember that you had arranged for the two of you to meet with his parents, who are known to frequent Hyde Park at the fashionable hour of five."

Udora jumped up. "Pistachions! And I must select something special to wear. Where does the time go?"

LADY EMILY AND LADY MARGARET arrived just over an hour later with young James sleeping sweetly in his mother's arms.

Lady Emily was in raptures. "Dear Yvette, I'm so happy to see you. This is the first time I've been out since the baby was born and I feel as if I've been set free." She settled her rose velvet skirt over the chair and untied the baby's bonnet. "I wasn't able to attend your concert at Lady Bancroft's unveiling of the Nash gazebo, but Lady Margaret tells me that you were marvellous." She smiled warmly. "We are so proud of you. I couldn't be happier for you if you were my own daughter."

Yvette folded her hands on her lap. "I owe my success to you, Lady Emily. I'll never forget that first day at Berrington House, when you caught me playing the pianoforte in the drawing room. *Nom de Dieu!* I thought surely you would give me my *congé.* Instead, you gave me the chance to sing at Lord Berrington's party."

Lady Margaret accepted a glass of fruit punch from the footman and raised it in a toast. "And now you are the darling of London Society."

Lady Udora lifted her own glass. "And I know that everyone agrees, Yvette, that it could not have happened to a more deserving person."

"*Merci,* you are far too kind. But it is you, Lady Emily, who are the fortunate one."

"Indeed. I must agree with you. I'm blessed with a loving husband, good friends, and a precious son. I've seen you watching him, Yvette. Would you care to hold him?"

"May I? I've been afraid to ask." And Yvette held out her arms.

OUTSIDE THE HOUSE Lord Bancroft handed the reins of his new black over to the stable-boy, who inspected the horse with the eye of an expert.

"Aye, and you've got yersel' a new mount, my lord. A right good nag 'e is, sir, but nothin' like the bay. You sell'im, my lord?"

Andrew's face darkened. "No, Timothy. You know I'd never sell Captain. The fact is, I lost him in a wager at White's."

"Blimey! Wot a powerful shame."

"Indeed. This one's name is Falcon."

The boy patted the horse's neck. "I like that. Birds' names is fittin' for horses. Anyways, those that flies like the wind.'' His freckled face split into a toothy grin. "Shall I hold 'im 'ere, my lord, or stable 'im wi' the others?''

"Put him in the stable, Timothy. I intend to stay for a while. Is that Lord Berrington's carriage?'' he asked, nodding towards the landau and pair of roans tied at a post beneath an oak tree.

"Aye. Been 'ere nigh on an 'our, they 'av.''

"Thank you.'' He flipped the youth a coin which Timothy caught before it stopped spinning. Andrew took the steps to the front door two at a time. He told himself he was a fool to come here now when he was so on edge. It wasn't just losing his best mount to Greebers and the fact that everyone at White's had taken a jab at him for his failure to "capture the Lark," as they put it.

The words which had passed between him and Yvette last night concerned him. If he had been a different kind of man, he could have simply led her to believe that he would offer for her. Instead, he had told her straight out that he loved her and wanted to be with her, but that marriage was out of the question. He was going to lose her if he wasn't careful. The knowledge brought his temper a peg closer to the boiling point.

Blowing out a deep breath, he lifted the knocker and let it fall. The door was immediately opened by the butler who seemed unusually flustered.

"Morning, McMasters,'' Andrew said handing him his beaver. "Tell mademoiselle that I wish to see her in the library.''

Douglas McMasters planted himself in the doorway. "My apologies, your lordship. Mademoiselle Cordé wishes me to say that she is not receiving today.''

"Balderdash!'' he snapped. "The Carstairs are here. Besides, her order does not apply to me, as you well know.''

"I'm afraid it does, sir. Mademoiselle mentioned your name in particular."

"Just do as I tell you." Andrew shot him a dark look. "And remember who got you this position. You and your wife were nothing but starving actors when I found you."

"I'm beholden to you, Lord Bancroft, but Mary and I are happy here. The mademoiselle knows that it was you who sent us round that first day, but she doesn't hold it against us."

"You told her? I gave you orders not to mention how the job came about."

"We didn't need to tell her, my lord. She guessed it from the start, but she said that seeing as how we did our work, she wouldn't hold it against us. She's a right fine woman for a Frenchie."

Andrew was fast losing what little temper he had left. "Out of my way, you ungrateful cullion." He attempted to push the butler aside, but McMasters stood fast.

The sound of their scuffle carried down the corridor to the library where Yvette was entertaining.

She stood up, holding the baby in her arms. "Please excuse me a moment, my ladies, while I see to the commotion in the hall."

Udora laughed. "It's probably Maggie having another confrontation with the cats. Would you like me to see to it?"

Yvette shook her head. "It's all right. I'm nearest the door." She nuzzled the baby's head with her chin. "Lady Emily, do you mind? I shan't be a moment and I can't bear to put the darling down."

ANDREW WAS ALREADY HALFWAY down the corridor when he saw Yvette coming down the hallway with the baby in her arms. He stopped in midstride and sucked in his breath.

By all that was holy! He had thought she was beautiful before, but standing there like a madonna, so serene and lovely, she shone with a radiance that brought tears to his eyes.

CHAPTER TWELVE

ANDREW OPENED HIS MOUTH to speak but found he was tongue-tied. It was Yvette who broke the spell.

"Lord Bancroft? What are you doing here? I told you that I could not go riding with you in the country."

He smiled lopsidedly. "I hoped that you would change your mind. May I be so bold as to say that you look most enchanting, standing there with the babe in your arms."

"*Merci*. Please, Andrew. You must excuse me. I have guests."

He came towards her, close enough that the scent of lavender tugged gently at his senses. He reached over and chucked the baby under the chin. Baby James wriggled in his blue shawl and grasped a lock of Yvette's hair in his pudgy hand.

She laughed. "Now see what you've done, little imp. You've **ma**de my hair come down." The baby laughed and cooed. Yvette tried to push her hair into place but it was impossible. She handed the baby to Andrew, who stiffened.

"It's all right, Andrew." A smile flashed across her face. "The baby won't break if you hold him."

"He's so small."

"Actually, he's quite big for his age. He has his father's eyes."

"And his mother's smile, though I never thought I'd admit it. Babies are supposed to be babies. Not replicas of their parents."

Yvette smiled as she arranged her hair into place. "You like holding him, don't you?"

"I think it's something I could get used to."

She held out her arms and he handed James back to her. "Yvette, I must talk to you."

"I don't think we have anything further to say to each other," Yvette said firmly. "We've said it all before."

"The feelings between us are too strong to extinguish with a few ill-chosen words, as we did last night. I am quite willing to wait for our conversation until your guests take their departure."

"Andrew, I don't think—"

"I won't let you say no," he broke in. "This is very important to me."

"Why, may I ask? Do you have another bet posted at White's?"

His face drained of colour. "So you heard about that."

"Is there anyone in London who has not?"

"It was a stupid thing to do. The bet was made before I came to know you. I strongly regretted it afterwards, but it was too late to repair the damage."

"You lost your horse?" She looked up.

"Yes."

"Good."

He winced. "Are you so vindictive?"

"Not usually, but it does my soul good to see you get a proper set-down for a change." She held out a little finger and the baby grasped it, chuckling.

He slapped his hand against his thigh. "For a change?" His voice had risen. "I've had nothing but set-downs since the day I first met you. You've unsettled me until I no longer know which way to turn."

"I'm sorry," she said stiffly. "I didn't mean to . . ."

Udora came to the door of the library and stopped. "Is everything all right, Yvette? Oh, good morning, Lord Bancroft. What a pleasant surprise."

He stepped forward and bowed. "Lady Udora. I see that Lady Emily is here."

"Yes, do you plan to join us? We are about to have coffee."

Yvette frowned at Udora, but she smiled. "I know Lady Emily and Lady Margaret will be pleased to see you."

"Thank you," he said. "The pleasure will be mine. I fully intended to call on Lord Berrington after the baby was born but unfortunately, I was away."

"Then do come into the library."

Andrew cast a triumphant look over his shoulder at Yvette, then stepped aside and ushered her in front of him. Yvette swept past him, marshalling all the pride she could summon.

As Udora predicted, Lady Emily and Lady Margaret were delighted to chat with Andrew and share his fascination with baby James. But they were hardly prepared when Andrew took the baby from Yvette and tucked him into the crook of his arm. A few significant looks darted among the three women as they watched the currents flow between Andrew and Yvette. A short time later Lady Emily winked and said that, regrettably, she must be leaving.

In what seemed like no time, Yvette and Udora were left alone with Andrew. Then Udora lifted the edge of her skirt and said in an overly loud voice, "Oh, pistachions! How careless of me. I must have got a drop of apricot jam from the tarts onto my skirt." She contrived to look almost innocent of guile. "Dear me, I hope you'll excuse me, Lord Bancroft. I really must change at once."

He smiled with ill-concealed relief and rose. "A pity, Lady Udora. I hope the stain will come out."

Yvette looked a scant shade above grim. "I hardly think it will be a problem. Even at the most generous, the stain would be considered infinitesimal."

Udora smiled. "A stain is a stain." She curtsied and sailed grandly towards the door. "So glad that you could join us, Andrew. We missed you dreadfully while you were away." She closed the door behind her.

SILENCE REIGNED in the library. Now that they were alone, Andrew felt the quiet settle like a cloak about his shoulders. He strode to the fireplace and warmed his hands. "I thought they would never leave. There is so much I want to say to you, Yvette."

"Then perhaps you had best begin. You cannot stay long. I am expecting another guest."

"Who, may I ask?"

"You may not," Yvette flashed.

"Then I shall remain here until he arrives and throw him out on his ear."

"Don't be despicable. If you must know, it is Lady Sedgeburry who is coming to buy the Chinese wedding chest."

"The black lacquered one from your sitting-room?"

"The same. I need the money to help with my final payment on the house."

"It will bring a paltry sum." He scowled. "Knowing your determination, I'm surprised you aren't trying to sell the painting."

"The thought occurred to me, but the chest will fetch more." The moment she said it, she realized her mistake, but it was too late.

Andrew turned upon her. "What the devil do you mean? The painting is a Bernard Chevalier. Why haven't you hung it over the fireplace as I suggested, instead of leaving it on the floor propped against the desk? If you will allow me, I would be pleased to show you how it will look." The tone of his voice made it sound more like an order than an offer of help.

Goaded beyond patience, Yvette glared at him. "I have no intention of hanging it there or in any other place. I hadn't planned to tell you this, but the painting is an imitation."

"The devil, you say. That is impossible." He picked up the painting and studied it carefully. "No, mademoiselle. I can swear to the fact that this is the same painting that has been in our family for nearly a quarter of a century."

"That may be true, my lord, but it is only a copy. Monsieur Chevalier was a friend of my father. The artist gave the painting to him in return for a favour and it hung on our wall for many years."

"I find that highly unlikely." He was still studying the picture.

"Have you ever known me to lie, Andrew?"

"No." He stormed across the room and then came back to stand beside her. "Why didn't you say something when my mother gave the painting to you last night?"

"What would I have gained by telling her?"

"I know there is no love lost between the two of you. And I know how much you depend on your performances to support your independence. You would have gained your fee, for one thing."

"But at what price?" Yvette asked quietly. "Your mother sets great store by the things she possesses." She looked away. "And there are other reasons."

"Such as?"

"Reasons I prefer to keep my own."

He took her by the shoulders and held her firmly in his grip. "Confound you, woman. One moment I think I have at last understood you, and the next moment you've opened the door to a new puzzle." His gaze softened. "But you are right about one thing. It would have stunned my mother to have the painting revealed as a fraud especially in public. Few people would have been so considerate of her feelings. Particularly when one considers how badly she has behaved towards you."

"I can understand her loyalty to her family."

His hands shook. "But I no longer can, my dearest." He bent his head and kissed her with growing passion.

Too caught up in the wonder of his embrace to think clearly, Yvette made no move to pull away. His strength, coupled with his gentleness, wooed her and she gave in to the yearnings that he had ignited with the touch of his hands.

He held her at arm's length and swore softly. Then, in one desperate move, he pulled her against him and kissed her cheeks, her forehead and her hair. Once again he found her lips and kissed her long and deeply. She felt herself slip into a place too sweet to leave.

It was only the cat Sinbad, rubbing against her leg, that brought her to her senses. "No, Andrew. No. We mustn't. It isn't right."

"How can it be wrong when it bespeaks paradise?"

"Please go now, before it is too late." She pushed him away, then bent down to pick up the cat and hold it protectively in front of her. "I need some time to think, Andrew."

"Very well. If that is your desire. May I return tonight?"

"So soon?" she asked, remembering that Udora would be away that evening. At the same time she wondered how she could make the time pass until she saw him again. She ran her fingers through the cat's fur to hide her shaking hands. "Yes, Andrew. Come tonight."

The breathlessness in her voice excited him until he was forced to knot his hands behind him. It was all he could do to keep from taking her into his arms just once more, but he knew it could be a fatal mistake. His voice was husky.

"The painting, Yvette. What do you intend to do with it?"

"You may have it if you like. There is no need to tell your mother that it is not genuine. Perhaps you can think of some believable excuse for my having returned it."

"Thank you. As to the payment on the house, please consider the debt cancelled. The house is yours alone."

Yvette gasped. "No! You cannot. I'm sure your only intention was to be generous, but I could never accept such a gesture. I shall have the money for you on the day it is due."

"Egad, Yvette." He shook his head in wonder, and she was surprised to see that his eyes were damp. "What am I to do about you, my sweet?" he said, then turned and strode out the door.

"And you, Andrew," she said, once he was out of sight, "what am I to do about you?"

She stood there for several minutes without moving until Sinbad, growing tired of her embrace, meowed to be put down.

THE AFTERNOON seemed to drag into days. Lady Sedge-burry came with her driver and bought the Chinese chest. Mr. Armbruster arrived to help plan the songs to be used for the musical evening at Marlborough House. Lady Udora primped and preened until Charles Willingsly arrived to take her driving in Hyde Park. They both tried, albeit rather feebly, to interest Yvette in accompanying them, but she refused. Their relief was almost unforgivably obvious.

As for Yvette, she attended to her duties and gave proper orders to her servants, all the while thinking about Andrew and remembering the loneliness of the past week while he was in the country. But she must face facts: the cold reality of her situation, his obligations to his family; the reactions of Society. She had thought that he was lost to her forever. In truth, after tonight he might well be.

With that appalling realization came her decision. She knew the time would come when she might regret it. Indeed, she probably would regret it, but sometimes the risk must prove worth the consequences. Tonight was her last chance. Before she could change her mind, she rang for Maggie and asked her to draw a bath.

HE ARRIVED PROMPTLY at the appointed time. If Yvette had thought he looked haggard after his return from the north, tonight he appeared ravaged. Although he was impeccably dressed, his eyes were overbright, and were accentuated by dark circles. For a man accustomed to being in control, Andrew was unusually nervous, moving from chair to window to bookcase, seemingly unable to sit still for more than a moment at a time.

Yvette could easily sympathize with him. Though her decision was made, she still had no idea how to tell him. Simply to blurt it out would be too forward. No, she must wait for the proper time. If it never came, then it would surely be a sign that she had been too hasty in making up her mind.

She stood and walked to a small table in front of the fireplace. "I've asked the cook to prepare a light repast. I hope you are hungry."

"I suppose I should be. I can't remember when I last ate."

Yvette motioned to the table as the butler entered with his tray. "You may put it here, McMasters."

"May I serve, mademoiselle?"

"No thank you. You may leave. I'll not need you again tonight."

He left and closed the door softly behind him. Andrew came over to hold Yvette's chair, then took the one opposite her. She lifted the lid of the tureen. "Green turtle soup. I seem to recall that you favour it. May I fill your bowl?"

"Please." He broke off a piece of crusty bread and spread it with a thick layer of butter.

Yvette ladled the steaming broth into her own bowl, taking as long as possible to perform the simple task. She had no wish to meet his gaze. He was far too adept at reading her thoughts.

She nearly jumped when he reached across the table and captured her hand. "Thank you for permitting me this time alone with you," he said. "I know how you feel about observing the proprieties, but sometimes feelings run too deep to be shared by a third party."

Yvette laughed nervously. "Lady Udora has been a blessing to me since I left Lord Berrington's house, but jewel that she is, she can be a bit overwhelming. I suppose that's why she makes a dependable chaperon."

He released her hand and leaned back in his chair. His gaze held hers and he shook his head. "Have you any idea what you have done to my life since I met you? Imagine, I have been here all of twenty minutes and I have yet to tell you how lovely you look. The truth is, I have run out of ways to describe my feelings.''

She blushed and laughed. ''I find that hard to imagine. But I've been wondering, Andrew, did you return the painting to your mother?''

''Yes, and I must beg your forgiveness for putting words into your mouth. I told her that I couldn't bear to part with the Chevalier, and that you had agreed to return it, with considerable regret.''

''Splendid. I hope she accepted the story.''

''Indeed she did. In a few days you will receive a necklace that is entirely lacking in sentimental virtue, but quite valuable. It is my hope that you will be able to sell it for enough money to pay all of your bills, including the balance which you owe on the house.''

Yvette forced a smile. ''And then you will have no need to call. Are you so eager to rid yourself of me?''

''I think you know better than that. But it is what you wish, is it not? To be beholden to no one?''

''It is *one* of the things I wish, at least.''

''Ah. Then there are others?'' He waited expectantly but she shrugged her shoulders and was silent. He pushed his soup plate aside, no longer willing to pretend to eat. ''Let me guess. You want a horse and carriage of your very own, jewels, a blue parasol trimmed with garlands of silk roses, and a white fur cape with a muff and bonnet to match.''

''Stop teasing. You know I care very little for the latest fashions. It is only thanks to Udora's insistence that I force myself to attend the shops.''

''Then what is it that you want most of all in the whole world, Yvette?''

The answer was easy. She wanted a family to call her own. But it could never be. Not now. She had made her decision. After tonight there would be no turning back.

She rose and walked to the music box which sat on a cherry-wood end table. "I think your question is too philosophical to pursue over green turtle soup."

"That may be, but I have yet to see you take the first spoonful."

"Nor have you," she pointed out.

"Could it be that we have other things on our minds?"

Her eyes twinkled. "Possibly. Things like what to wear to the party at Marlborough House, what entertainment to provide for my Thursday salon, what plants to choose for the herb garden."

He laughed. "You are not even close to guessing what was on my mind."

"No?" she asked, winding the screw on the music box. When she released it the porcelain lord and lady who adorned it twirled to the sensuous music of a waltz.

He stood and came over to take her hand. "On second thought, perhaps you *do* know what I was thinking, but you are reluctant to admit it. May I have this dance, mademoiselle?"

She inclined her head and curtsied to his bow. Before she had time to catch her breath he had swept her into the magic of the dance.

They whirled about the room, laughing, more often than not, when they came dangerously close to bumping the furniture. Yvette was giddy with excitement. She threw back her head and hummed a line or two of the song. Andrew responded by executing an intricate twirl which brought them closer together, so close that she could feel the movement of his thighs as he stepped forward and then back. His gaze met hers and held it captive. It was all she could do to breathe, but she heard him inhale in short, quick breaths.

Then as the music wound down, he slowed his steps until they were scarcely moving at all. His eyes never left her face. She was lost in the depths of a gaze so compelling that it pushed all thoughts of modesty and propriety completely from her mind. All she could think of was what it might be like to belong to him body and soul.

When the last note died away leaving the room in silence, Yvette was afraid that the pounding of her heart would betray her.

Andrew stood there holding her in his arms, as if he couldn't bring himself to let her go. He shook his head. "Why is it that the music always ends too soon?"

She smiled. "Any longer, Andrew, and you would be quite out of breath."

"The music has little to do with the state of my breathlessness, as you well know."

"Indeed? Then could it be that old age is creeping up on you?" When he scowled, she laughed merrily. "Perhaps not. Then could it be that this is the first time you have waltzed with a French woman alone in the privacy of her home?"

He brushed a kiss onto her forehead. "It is the first time I have danced with you. I mean *truly* danced, without an audience of hundreds watching for our first fall from grace."

Yvette looked up at him. "Hmmm. This . . . fall from grace. It sounds serious."

"Only to those who claim the right to dictate to others."

"I think we may have already committed our first sin against Society by meeting here alone in the library. I think perhaps it was a mistake on my part. Does it not concern you, Andrew?'' She was serious as she asked the question.

"Only if it concerns you. I must confess that it does surprise me that Udora has not yet made her presence known."

"She is meeting Charles and his family this evening."

He tensed. "Indeed? A sudden change of plans, I presume. Otherwise she would have been here to chaperon you."

"No." Yvette spoke simply.

"No? Are you saying that you already knew of her plans when you agreed to let me see you tonight?"

"Yes."

He blew his breath out in a slow stream. "Do you know that, in the eyes of Society, you might easily have compromised yourself, in spite of the fact that your servants are nearby?"

"I've sent them to bed." She heard his quick intake of breath and felt his hands tense on her shoulders.

"Yvette . . ." His voice was strained and deep.

"Yes, Andrew."

"Egad!" He turned quickly and strode towards the windows, then back to her side. "Yvette, don't play games with me. There was a time when I enjoyed our little sparring matches. It didn't matter then who came out ahead and who was left to eat crow. But now things have gone too far for me to be content with mere words between us."

"This is no game. If you but ask, you will find I am quite ready to do your bidding."

"You are what?" He appeared thunderstruck.

"Don't pretend you didn't hear me. And why should you be surprised? You told me once that you always get your way." She curtsied low and long. "Very well, Lord Bancroft. You have won."

"No." There was desperation in his voice. "No, I don't believe you. You're still playing some kind of game, mademoiselle. But you haven't told me the rules."

She took his face in her hands. "Believe me, Andrew. It's as simple as this: I don't want to lose you. If the only way I can be with you is by becoming your mistress, then I am quite prepared to do so."

He shook his head. "You would do that for me, knowing the consequences?"

She nodded. "I know that it can be only temporary. For this I swear, Andrew: once you marry, as I know you must, it shall be over between us. I could not bring myself to lie with another woman's husband." He was about to speak, but she touched her fingers to his lips. "There is one more condition: that you come to me as my guest, and not as my provider, for I will accept nothing from you. Nothing, except your affection."

His eyes blazed. "Affection? Do you dare insult me by calling what I feel for you *affection?* Have you no understanding of the torment I suffered while I was away? I love you, Yvette. I love you more than life itself. I shall always love you."

"As I love you, Andrew. I only wish to ease the pain of our loss."

"By all that is holy..." He paced twice across the room and back before he could speak. "Then there shall be no loss. I'll never let you go, Yvette. Never. Marry me. Be my wife in the true sense of the word." Yvette stared at him in disbelief but she saw only truth in his eyes. He had asked her to marry him. And he meant it. She was too dumbstruck to answer immediately.

Andrew took her hesitation as an acceptance and pulled her into his arms. Their kiss was wild and warm and wonderful, and for those few splendid moments it seemed that nothing on earth could ever come between them. She wound her arms round his shoulders and cupped his neck in the palm of her hand. Her lips found his and she kissed him with sweet abandon.

He gloried in the feeling of power that she gave to him. It appalled him that he could have waited so long to offer for her. Now that it was done, he had only faint qualms about breaking the news to his mother. In time she would come to love Yvette for the strength and goodness of her spirit.

Andrew slid his hands down Yvette's back to hold her more intimately. She tensed and pressed her hands against his chest.

"No, Andrew. I'm sorry if I've misled you. I can't. I just can't."

"You can't?" He made an effort to get a grip on his raging emotions. "Of course not, my love. Forgive me for my haste. I understand it is your wish to wait until we are married."

Her voice came in a whisper. "No. I mean that I can't marry you."

"You can't marry me! I don't believe you. But why?" He held her at arm's length frowning in his effort to understand. "It's my mother, isn't it? You're afraid that she'll change my mind once she learns that I have asked for your hand in marriage." He threaded his fingers through her hair and held her head between his hands. "Trust me, my love. My mother will give us her blessing once she knows she has no choice. For all her rigid control, my mother wants me to be happy as much as she wants to preserve the family name."

He saw the tears form on Yvette's lashes and she blinked. "No, Andrew, it isn't your mother who stands in the way of our marriage. It's me. It's who I am. Or who I was. Please, I beg of you not to ask me about it now.''

He studied her face before he answered. "All right. I will not ask you now, if you insist. But my offer still stands. I want to marry you.''

"The answer is no, regrettably.'' She raised her eyes to meet his. "But I am willing to be your mistress for as long as you will have me.''

He stared at her for a frighteningly long moment as sweat beaded his upper lip. Then he pushed her away, slapped his hand against his thigh and strode to the door, turning at the last instant to fix her with his gaze.

"And *my* answer is no, Yvette. I will not take you as a mistress. I want you to consider my offer of marriage before you make up your mind. If you need time to do so, the time is yours.'' He wiped his hand across his mouth. "I shall not see you again until I arrive to escort you to the party at Marlborough House, at which time I shall expect an answer.''

"But I...'' There was no need to finish. He had already closed the door behind him.

CHAPTER THIRTEEN

AFTER ANDREW HAD LEFT so abruptly, Yvette climbed the stairs to her bedchamber. Never had the house seemed so empty. Never had her life been so devoid of hope. She reminded herself over and over that Andrew loved her, that he wanted to marry her. But the knowledge made losing him even more painful. If only she could marry him and forget the past as if it had never happened. But she couldn't do that. Eventually he would want to know exactly who she was, and why she was in fear for her life. She could not lie to him and she could not marry him if she told the truth.

It was too early to fall asleep and Udora still had not returned home. Yvette thought once she heard her at her door but it proved to be Ulysses and his twin, Odysseus, scratching to be let into her room. She sat down on the bed and joined the two tabby cats in a game of hide-beneath-the-covers. If nothing else, it was distracting. After a while, Yvette tired of playing with them and sat down in a chair to read the latest novel by Miss Jane Austen.

It was the sound of tearing paper which brought her back from her rendezvous with the elegant Mr. Darcy. "No, no, you bad boys," Yvette said, jumping up to take the journal away from the cats. "Now look what you've done. You've torn the back from Mr. Wolgren's diary."

She was about to put the book down when she discovered a secret pocket between the leather cover and the binding. "Ah, what's this?" she said aloud. There were dozens of small sheets of foolscap stuffed into the pocket. Yvette carefully withdrew them and spread them out on the bed. Ulysses batted one of the pieces of paper, rolled over on his back and wrestled with it until Yvette snatched it from him and held it under the light from the lamp.

At first it appeared to be a series of numbers, but she soon realized that they were receipts for markers, signed acknowledgements of debt. The vowels were made out for various amounts of money, some of them quite considerable, and each one bore the signature of Archibald Wolgren.

Breathlessly, Yvette shooed the cats from the bed and collected the markers into a neat stack. "Now," she said aloud, "we shall see if what I am thinking could possibly be true." Her hands shook with excitement as she went to her writing desk, took out a piece of paper and a pencil and began to add up the figures. The column was long. Her nervousness forced her to start over twice, but when she finally made the tally, the sum was exactly what she had expected. It was the amount of money that Wolgren had accused her father of embezzling from the Poole Shipping Company.

Yvette fought back her tears. It had taken years, had cost the lives of her family, as well as their fortune, and it had nearly destroyed her one chance at happiness. But it was here: the evidence she needed to clear her father's name. Each marker was dated, and the dates coincided with the dates her father was said to have stolen the money.

For all these years the proof of her father's innocence had lain in the personal journal of the man who had accused him. They both had paid dearly for Mr. Wolgren's addiction to gambling. Wolgren had been killed in the duel and her father had died because he fled to France to avoid prosecution.

And yet someone was still watching her, someone who had vowed vengeance and thought that she knew where the embezzled money was hidden.

SHE WAS STILL SITTING on the bed with the markers clutched to her bosom when Udora tapped on the door and came in.

"Yvette Cordé! Whatever are you doing? Have you gone mad or merely entered a kind of trance?"

"Not Yvette Cordé," she said softly. "Yvette Claudine Françoise Bouvier."

"What? Great heavens!" Udora tapped the side of her head with the palm of her hand. "I knew I shouldn't have accepted a second glass of brandy. I'm so foxed I can't think straight. Whatever are you raving about?" she said, dropping into a chair and kicking her slippers across the room.

Yvette tucked the markers into the journal and pulled a shawl about her shoulders. "You said once that we must have a serious chat."

Udora yawned again. "An excellent idea, dear, but certainly not now. My head is too muzzy for anything to get through it. Might it wait until tomorrow?" She shuddered. "You can't believe the indignities I suffered at the hand of Charles's mother. She all but called me a harridan. Can you imagine that?"

"I'm so sorry. Does that mean that Charles will be less inclined to court you?"

She yawned again. "Give me credit for my charms, Yvette. Suffice it to say that Charles is shaping up rather nicely. I've about decided to take him on as Number Five."

Yvette grinned and clasped her hands together in delight. "How enchanting! Has he offered for you?"

"Not as yet, but he will, if and when I grant him the opportunity. Frankly, I've been holding off until I can think of someone equally as capable, who might take over for me as your companion."

"Oh, but you mustn't let that hold you back. I could manage by myself, if need be."

"Pistachions! You'd spend every night alone in your house with nothing but the servants and a book to keep you company. Just as you did tonight."

"I was not alone."

"Don't say things when I'm too foxed to think." Udora looked appalled. "Surely you didn't compromise your reputation by entertaining a man?"

Suddenly Yvette was reluctant to continue the discussion. So much had happened in the last few hours that it could only be to her advantage to allow a little time for the events to settle in her mind.

"I thought you knew me better than that, Udora." She stood and went to the armoire for her night-dress. "Am I the kind of woman to flout convention?"

"Of course not."

"So nice of you to say so. Now, if you have no objection, I should like to retire."

"No objection at all, my dear. I am quite flaggy myself."

BY THE NEXT MORNING Udora had forgotten all about the little chat that Yvette had promised her. Charles had come to call on her at the scandalous hour of ten. Udora thought it was delightfully cheeky of him and, despite her throbbing head, asked the cook to serve up breakfast in the garden.

Yvette attended to her correspondence and made plans to find the most beautiful gown possible for the Marlborough House ball. That afternoon she shopped at Singleton's on Mount Street and discovered a bolt of ivory lace over iridescent pink, green and gold Chinese silk. She draped it over her arm and when she moved, it was like clouds drifting across a rainbow. She gasped when she heard the price. It was far less costly than she had imagined, yet nothing she had seen could equal its beauty.

From there she went to Harrington's, Lady Margaret's establishment, to be measured for the gown. The seamstresses, as a special favour to Yvette, promised to have it ready within the week.

Twice she thought she had been followed, but when she turned to take a better look, she could see nothing untoward. It occurred to her that somehow she would have to come to terms with her pursuer, if indeed there really was one. Now, at least, she could, if necessary, take the proof of her father's innocence to a solicitor. When she revealed that it was Wolgren who had embezzled the money and lost it, it would surely put an end to the business of vengeance. She would be able to relax at last.

The question was how and when to reveal the plot against her father. To do so could hurt Andrew's family, despite the fact that their relationship to Archibald Wolgren was remote.

It was the afternoon of the third day after Andrew had offered for her, when the package arrived by special messenger. Yvette and Udora had just bid their guests adieu and had settled down with the cats and a cup of tea in the library, when McMasters tapped at the door and handed over the tissue-wrapped package.

"Did the messenger say who it was from?" Yvette asked.

"No, miss. I was told you will find a card inside the box."

"Open it, open it," Udora said, clapping her hands. "Oh, how I do enjoy surprises."

Yvette untied the blue velvet ribbon and slid the paper from the rectangular box. Inside was a necklace and matching earrings of diamonds, opals and pearls in an ornate gold-link setting. Yvette lifted it and held it against her gown.

Udora looked impressed. "I must confess it is rather ornate, but, my dear, I suspect it's worth a considerable fortune, assuming the stones are real," she said dryly. "Quick, read the card."

Yvette searched through the layers of tissue and found a small envelope. She opened the card and read aloud the unfamiliar handwriting.

"My dear Mademoiselle Cordé,
My son tells me that you have been kind enough to return the painting by Bernard Chevalier. I had no idea that Andrew was so sentimentally attached to it. It is my sincere hope that you will accept in exchange, the necklace and eardrops contained herein."

The letter was signed by Lady Bancroft. When Yvette saw the expression on Udora's face, her own smile turned to a look of surprise. "What? What is it, Udora? The jewels seem to be quite authentic."

"Just when did you return the painting to Lord Bancroft? I know for certain he hasn't been here for three days." She punctuated the air with her finger. "It was he who called the night I visited with Charles's family, wasn't it? You thought I was too far into my cups to catch on to it.''

Yvette blushed. "I assure you, nothing improper transpired. If you must know, Andrew asked me to marry him.''

"He didn't!" Udora openly gaped.

"He did. I know you won't understand this, but I was forced to refuse him.''

"Pistachions, you say. You must be out of your mind!" Udora sank back in her chair. "I can't believe you would refuse him, considering how hard I've worked to bring the two of you together.'' She picked up the jewels and ran them through her fingers, smoothing the opals with her thumbs. "You must be heartbroken, my dear, but I know you well enough to realize you must have a good reason. Though to me the only logical excuse would be that you had already passed on to your just reward.''

She returned the necklace to the box and placed both hands on the arms of her chair. "You said something about having a talk with me, Yvette. Perhaps this would be a good time.''

Yvette clasped her hands together on her lap and leaned forward. "I suppose we must. It will all come out one day, whether I plan it that way or not.''

IT WAS MORE THAN an hour later when Yvette had fully described all the details of her father's flight from London to France. Udora was uncharacteristically quiet, so engrossed was she in the revelations. She broke into Yvette's monologue with a question or two to clarify certain points, but for the most part she sat wide-eyed and attentive.

Finally Yvette leaned back against the chair and spread her hands. "My father was executed by one of Napoleon's generals, because he was mistakenly believed to be spying for the English. Afterwards, my mother and I secretly booked passage on a trading vessel and returned to England. Even though she had been born here, she had no family left, but it seemed safer than remaining in France."

Yvette fixed her gaze on her lap. "She became ill and died ten months later. Our holdings in Lyons had been confiscated. What little money we had taken with us was nearly gone. I had no choice but to find suitable employment."

"It was then that you went to work as a maid at Berrington House?"

"Yes. The brother-in-law of the man my father killed in the duel vowed to find me and force me to return the stolen money. Money that had all gone for the gambling debts incurred by Mr. Wolgren."

"But can't you go to the authorities and have this man apprehended?"

"I have no proof of his threats. The letter was lost during our flight to London. Nor am I certain of his name or appearance."

"Then he hasn't tried to find you?"

"I don't know." Yvette moved restlessly. "Several times I have thought I was being followed, but it could have been my imagination."

"Indeed." Udora reached for Yvette's hand and squeezed it. "You poor dear. What you must have suffered. Let me speak to some friends of mine. With this new evidence, I'm sure we can publicly clear your father's name."

"Not yet, Udora. I can't face the notoriety. First I must get through the ordeal of the party at Marlborough House."

"All right. If you insist. But at least you know you are not alone in this."

THE DAYS WHICH FOLLOWED were fraught with the tension of preparation for the Marlborough House ball. Added to that there was the Thursday night salon to be got through. Much as she usually enjoyed them, Yvette now dreaded the crush of people. She spent the evening looking for Andrew, but he didn't put in an appearance.

The dressmakers at Harrington's finished Yvette's gown the night before the ball and it was everything she had dreamed it would be. As she dressed for the party the next night, Udora came into her room.

She stopped short and took Yvette's hand, turning her round. "*C'est ravissante!* This is by far the most exciting gown you have ever worn."

"*Merci bien.*" Yvette lifted the free-flowing panels which drifted over the narrow skirt. "It was designed by Lady Margaret. She said she adapted it from a picture in *La Belle Assemblée*. Such talent she has...and such generosity. But you!" she said, looking at Udora. "You look magnificent. Is this a new gown?"

Udora twirled round until the blue, green and silver beads shimmered like tiny droplets of water over and about her soft curves "I bought it the week after my last husband's funeral. Of course I couldn't wear it until I took off the black gloves, and then I just couldn't find the right occasion to wear such a significant gown as this." She laughed. "But I think Charles is worth it."

"You are smitten, I do believe. Is Charles going to ride in Andrew's carriage with us?"

"No. I told him that Lord Bancroft would see to our transport. Charles will meet us there, since he lives nearby."

Yvette smoothed the long, snug-fitting gloves up over her elbows. "I wish we didn't have to go. I have a bad feeling about tonight."

"Nonsense. I heard you rehearsing your music earlier today with Mr. Armbruster. Your voice has never been more exquisite. And by-the-by, Charles tells me that after the other guests depart, the four of us have been invited by the duke to remain behind for a more intimate party with some of the house guests."

"*Nom de Dieu!* Just when I want nothing more than to leave early."

"Pistachions! It's just your feeling of apprehension. It will disappear as soon as the music begins." She winked. "If you like, I shall make it a point to turn my back if you wish a second dance with Andrew."

Yvette laughed in spite of herself. "Sometimes I think it is I who should be the chaperon instead of you."

ANDREW, LORD BANCROFT, arrived promptly at the appointed hour to escort the women to Marlborough House. If Yvette expected him to look the tragic lover, she was disappointed. There was a polite calmness, a self-confidence about him that both surprised and puzzled her. He had vowed that tonight she must give him the answer to his proposal. Was he so certain that she would accept...or had he already regretted his impulsiveness and decided to withdraw his offer?

Whatever his determination, Yvette made sure that Udora was at her side from the moment he arrived. She was not prepared to face Andrew alone, or to allow him an opportunity to quiz her.

She realized later that she needn't have concerned herself. The ballroom was already crowded by the time they arrived and passed through the receiving line. Charles

Willingsly attached himself to Udora's arm the moment she was announced. Mr. Armbruster had prevailed upon a footman to inform Yvette that he was ready and waiting in an anteroom, for her performance was to begin within the hour.

Yvette and Andrew were immediately surrounded by admirers: dowagers seeking to enhance their daughters' prospects with an eligible bachelor, and hot-handed rakes hoping for a dance or, at the very least, a chat with the Lark from Lyons.

Yvette turned to Andrew. "I am most grateful that you have brought us to the ball, but please do not feel obligated to look after me. Udora is near enough to satisfy the dictates of propriety."

He took her hand and placed it on his arm. "I shall not leave your side. Lest you have forgotten, I am expecting your answer tonight."

"Andrew, please don't make this more difficult than it is." Seeing that they were being closely watched, she forced a smile. It was intercepted by an exotic-looking man with dark eyes and sleek black hair caught in a short braid at the back of his head. He started towards them, his eyes riveted on Yvette.

She sucked in her breath. Was this the man? His face looked oddly familiar. Was he the one who had been following her?

Andrew felt her stiffen. "What is it? What's wrong?"

"Nothing. I . . . I need some air."

By that time the man had reached her side. He bowed, placing his palm upon his forehead in a salaam. "Mademoiselle. It would give me the greatest pleasure if you would grant me a place upon your dance card."

Andrew scowled. "Regrettably, the mademoiselle's card is already filled."

"I . . . I'm so sorry," Yvette said. When he was gone she hissed at Andrew, "That was a bald-faced lie. I haven't even begun to fill my card, since we only just arrived."

"Then let us proceed to the ballroom. The orchestra has begun another set." Without waiting for her response he covered her hand with his where it rested on his sleeve, guided her to the adjoining room, and swept her onto the dance floor.

"There is something I think you ought to know before you see my mother tonight."

"She is here?"

"Of course. The duke sent his carriage for her. Don't interrupt. I think you should know that I told my mother about the painting."

"You didn't! Was that wise? She must have been crushed."

"Only for the moment. I also told her that I am going to marry you."

Yvette looked up at him disbelievingly. He looked exceedingly happy and self-assured. "You shouldn't have done that, Andrew. I have already refused you."

He held her at arms' length and turned her in a pirouette, then pulled her close as the music swelled. "I won't accept your refusal, Yvette. We are destined to be together."

"And what about your family? Can you so easily cast aside the standards that have been set for you?"

"Everything must eventually change. If I believed for a moment that you didn't love me, I would not force this issue, but, my dearest, you *do* love me as I love you."

She was silent, pretending to concentrate on the dance.

"Say it, Yvette."

She saw the love in his eyes and knew that it was mirrored in her own. "Yes, Andrew. I do love you. But there is something I must tell you before we proceed."

"I am always willing to listen, but nothing you say can make a difference. Shall we find a secluded nook and talk about it? Over there behind the potted palm, perhaps?"

Yvette looked about them as the music slowed to a stop. Was she creating a fantasy out of her own imagination or was everyone watching Andrew and her when they left the dance floor? Snippets of conversation carried across the room as easily as feathers in the wind. The feeling that she was being watched grew increasingly oppressive. "I wonder," she asked, "could we find more privacy in the garden?"

He raised an eyebrow. "I would have suggested it but I thought . . ."

"To be sure, I must advise Lady Udora of my intentions."

He smiled. "Of course."

They found Udora and Charles chatting cosily beside a fernery. "Would you come with us to the garden?" Yvette asked. "I must speak to Lord Bancroft in private."

Udora gave her a significant look and nodded, taking Charles's hand and leading the way.

The night air was refreshing compared to the stuffiness of the Grand Salon. The sweet fragrance of roses mingled with the heady scent of lavender and wall-flowers as they strolled down the path towards a towering fountain which cast a dazzling spray in the light of the torches. Yvette found a seat on the edge of the fountain, closed her fan and let it dangle at her wrist.

Udora sent her a questioning glance then at Yvette's nod, fluttered her hand toward a stone bench a short distance away. "We'll be just over there, should you wish to speak to us."

Yvette squeezed Udora's hand and murmured a thank-you. A dozen or so couples had chosen to take the air but most of them had gathered in the gazebo which was set back among the trees and was lighted with a colourful display of Chinese lanterns.

Andrew stood facing Yvette, one foot resting upon the coping while he studied her face in the flickering light. The cascading spray of water muffled the voices of passers-by. He started to reach for her hands but she pulled back. "No, Andrew. This is difficult enough. Please do not distract me."

She looked up to see another group of people coming down the pathway. In a few minutes there would be no privacy at all. She clutched her hands in her lap and spoke haltingly.

"I told you once before that you knew nothing about me...about where I came from or who I am."

"It doesn't matter. It's who you are now..."

"No. You must hear this from me."

"Perhaps we should wait," he said, dreading to hear what she had to say, yet wanting to know all about her. His voice grew husky. "It has waited this long, my love. Tomorrow is soon enough."

Her heart thudded at his endearment. "No, Andrew. I cannot wait any longer. I must tell you now. I am not who you think I am. My real name is..."

"Mademoiselle Yvette Bouvier?" The man's harsh voice cut through the murmur of voices and the splash of water, bringing the conversations to an abrupt halt.

Yvette gasped and stood up. Her hands flew to her face demonstrating her fear.

The man was foxed, judging by the way he staggered across the narrow parapet that separated them. Other than the black hair spiked with grey which curled round his chubby face, there was nothing remarkable about him. Until one saw his eyes. Right now they were focussed upon Yvette with an intensity that radiated hatred like a tangible force.

Andrew confronted him. "See here, my good man. This is Mademoiselle Cordé. You have the wrong woman. Suppose you return to the house before you fall down."

"Who are you?" Yvette asked stiffly. "Are you the man who has been following me?" She fixed him with her gaze. "I remember you. You once tried to force your attentions upon me when I first came to London."

"I've chased you and your family from England to France and back again. The name's Clifford Waxton. My brother-in-law was Archibald Wolgren, the man from whom your father stole ten thousand pounds and then shot to death under the guise of a duel."

Yvette pressed her hands together in front of her and tried to keep her voice steady. "You are mistaken, monsieur."

"There's no mistake. When I approached you not long after you arrived in England it was only to be sure I had the right woman. I thought then that I was wrong but time has proven me correct. Do you deny that you are Yvette Bouvier?"

She glanced appealingly at Andrew, then back at the intruder. Her knees trembled and her mouth felt coated with cotton-wool when she spoke. "It . . . it is true, I am Yvette Bouvier, but my father was innocent of any wrongdoing. And I can prove it."

"Liar! Liar!" he snarled. His face turned a deep crimson and he lunged at her as if to strike her. She stumbled backward against the coping and would have fallen had it not been for Andrew, who caught her arm. But her hair was drenched in the cascading water.

The noise had attracted a crowd of onlookers who pushed forward to assist Andrew in restraining the man. Udora elbowed her way to Yvette's side. She took one look at her charge and cried out.

"Saints in heaven! What has he done to you? Is that blood on your forehead?"

"I don't think so." Yvette touched her face where the water trickled down from her hair. Her hand came away stained with black dye. "*Mon Dieu!* My hair. What am I to do?"

A trio of footmen arrived to detain Waxton, who continued to struggle violently, all the while shouting obscenities. "You've not heard the last of this! I'll make you give back the money your father stole!"

Someone told the footmen to take him to a private room and hold him until the runners arrived.

Yvette mopped at her face with a lace handkerchief. "Andrew," she wailed, "I'm so sorry to have embarrassed you."

His voice was tight. "Hush. Don't think about it now. We must get you inside."

Her words rushed forth in an unstoppable torrent. "The truth is that there never *was* any money. Wolgren gambled the money away, and to cover the theft, accused my father of embezzling the funds. He hoped to cover his tracks by killing my father in a duel, but instead, it was he who was killed."

"My dear. I had no idea," Andrew said softly. "Try not to think about it now. What's important is your safety. We must get you away from here," Andrew said as he put his arm protectively around her shoulders and guided her briskly towards the house.

Someone pushed forward. "Is it true, mademoiselle? Do you have proof? And are you really the daughter of Antoine Bouvier?"

"I... Yes." She looked up at Andrew, determined to tell him. "My father was a French nobleman, a son of the Comte Calvert de Lyons."

Andrew looked first stunned, then bewildered. "So this is what has been troubling you! Why didn't you tell me? My God, woman! Am I such an ogre that you feared—" He swore roundly. "What are we to do? Shall I take you home?"

"Don't be absurd," Udora sputtered. "She can hardly walk back through the Grand Salon with her face running black and brown."

Someone pushed through the crowd. "Here," said a brisk voice. "Let me, I know just the place to repair the damage."

"Mother!" Andrew said. His surprise was reflected in that one word.

She unwound her filmy gold shawl and covered Yvette's hair. "That should do until we can take care of it. Come with me." Her demeanour left no room for discussion.

Yvette and Udora followed her through a side entrance of the house to a bedchamber where a basin and pitcher of warm water was already waiting.

Yvette said in a small voice. "This is very kind of you, Lady Bancroft."

"Kindness has nothing to do with it. I could scarcely allow my son to become involved in this... this comic opera."

Yvette was close to tears. "I am so sorry. I do apologize for anything I may have done to embarrass you or your family, your ladyship."

"Indeed. But it is a little late for that, isn't it?"

Udora poured water into the basin. "Pistachions! I find this discussion nothing short of ludicrous. If Yvette were a domestic pretending to be noble, then there might be cause for embarrassment. But since the reverse is true, one might be wise to consider the implications before one passes judgement."

Lady Bancroft shifted her gaze to Udora. Her eyes glittered with grudging respect. "Yes. First things first." She pushed Yvette over to the wash-basin and motioned for her to begin. "For now, we must deal with this river of mud running down your face. What is it, mademoiselle? Have you dyed your hair?"

"Yes, I..."

Udora clapped her hands in delight. "Great pistachions! So you're a blonde underneath that ugly dye. You might have told me." She sniffed. "I never thought that your hair went well with your face." She sent the maid for another pitcher of water. "I suppose we must inform the duchess that you will be unable to sing tonight."

Lady Bancroft pressed her fingertips together. "Nonsense! That would be most unwise. Her Grace wields enormous influence. Besides, I know how much she has been counting on Mademoiselle Cordé to entertain. We cannot simply turn tail and run."

Yvette wrung the soap from her hair and looked up. "But how can I stand up there and sing? They will never stop laughing at me...or my dripping hair."

Lady Bancroft stood back and surveyed the situation. "You would look well in a turban, and they are quite in vogue. May I offer my shawl, since it matches the colours in your gown?''

"Splendid idea," Udora said.

Yvette studied the viscountess's face to see if there was some ulterior motive for her change of character. The woman gave her a quelling look, one shade above grim. "Yes, I know what you are thinking."

"I wonder why you are being so kind to me?"

"Especially when I have treated you so harshly in the past? I'm beginning to think perhaps I may have misjudged you, though I assure you, my dear, I would do anything, *anything* to protect my family." She lifted her chin in a defiant gesture. "When Andrew told me how you had protected our good name over the painting, I realized that there was more to you than a beautiful face and an exquisite voice. I want you to know that I very nearly considered giving Andrew my blessing to marry you, even before I learned that you sprang from noble blood."

"I . . . don't know what to say." Yvette gazed blankly at the viscountess.

"Say nothing. You mustn't assume that I approve of the marriage. You are hardly my first choice of daughter-in-law. But all things considered, I must bow to my son's wishes. In a day or two we shall meet so I may discover more about you and the unsavoury circumstances which brought you to this unfortunate state."

Udora's eyes narrowed. "How gracious of you. I shall certainly encourage my charge to consider your kind *invitation,* though in all honesty, I must assure you that his lordship has already made his feelings quite clear." Her voice rose as she realized their advantage. "However, we are admittedly curious about your own background, Lady Bancroft. Was it not Archibald Wolgren, your own cousin, I believe, who falsified evidence about his embezzlement?

Surely you are aware that it was he who forced Yvette's father to duel. Not the other way round.''

Lady Bancroft paled and would have spoken, but Yvette straightened up, tossing a spray of water across the room. "Please. Must we discuss this now? If I'm going to perform tonight we must not be at odds with one another. I need both of you."

Udora, looking only slightly repentant, wound the scarf over Yvette's hair and stood back. "You're right, of course. I'm sure we both owe you an apology." She spread her hands. "There. Rather good, I think, but it does need something."

Lady Bancroft unhooked a diamond clasp from her coronet of braids and pinned it to the turban. "Perfect! Wouldn't you say, ladies?" Her smile was a trifle forced.

They agreed that Yvette looked perfectly stylish. Lady Bancroft looked pleased, if painfully so. She clamped her arms against her sides as if attempting to contain her true feelings. "Now then, suppose we enter the arena? Take my arms, and smile, ladies, smile. Act as if this were just a lark."

Udora stopped in midstride and began to laugh. "My dear Lady Bancroft, I do believe you've just made a joke."

Lady Bancroft looked down her nose. "It was not intended as such."

Along with a crowd of curious bystanders, Andrew was waiting just outside the door. His thoughts were in a turmoil. Could he be dreaming? Was Yvette truly the daughter of Antoine Bouvier?

He had a fleeting memory of the scandal involving one of his distant relatives. Hadn't there been a pistol duel at dusk in Packer's Woods? Then a private funeral on a cold, drizzly afternoon? He remembered there'd been a search for the man who survived.

But Archibald Wolgren had been a bad hat who would have cozened his own mother out of her last crust of bread. The search for his killer and the missing money had been short-lived. Or so everyone had thought—everyone apparently, except for Yvette and the man who had pursued her.

Andrew felt the sweat begin to trickle down his temples. But why hadn't Yvette confided in him? He was an easy man to talk to. Kind, considerate to those less fortunate. She had had nothing to fear from him. Why had she not spoken?

Even as the thought crossed his mind he was chagrined to remember the times they had fought over trivialities. He knew instinctively that she enjoyed their verbal fisticuffs as much as he did. But this was different. If she loved him as she claimed to, then nothing was too terrible to hold back. The thought frightened him and he was glad when someone approached to tell him that the runners had removed the intruder to the local constabulary.

At the sound of a commotion Andrew turned toward the corridor. The last thing in the world he expected to see coming towards him was the three women, laughing light heartedly as they strolled arm in arm. He pulled his handkerchief from his coat and mopped his brow.

A low murmur of astonishment rippled across the room punctuated by hearty applause. Lady Bancroft approached her son. "Really, Andrew, don't stand there like a fish gasping for air. Close your mouth."

Yvette smiled tentatively and dropped a curtsy. "I believe I promised you the next dance."

Andrew stared at his mother, who nodded, and then at Yvette. Their gaze met and held for an excruciatingly long moment. He bowed slowly and offered his arm. "Will you do me the honour, Mademoiselle Bouvier?"

She inclined her head, her gaze never once leaving his, and spoke just above a whisper. "The honour is mine, Lord Bancroft."

He swept her into his arms and guided her to the centre of the floor. "What happened in there? My mother looks as if she's come unstarched. And the three of you cavorting like bosom-bows." He shook his head as if to clear it.

"Hardly that," Yvette replied demurely. "We merely put on a show to save face. I can explain."

His face looked grim. "I hope so! I'd say quite a number of things need to be explained."

"I'm sorry, Andrew. I'll tell you everything if you will but give me a chance." She sighed. "But can you ever forgive me for not confiding in you? I felt my life depended upon it."

He didn't answer for a moment, but then they were busy executing a series of dips and turns until Yvette was quite breathless. When she lifted her face to his, he saw the pain in her eyes and he knew he was lost, no matter what she had done.

"Forgive you, Yvette? I don't know." The smile in his eyes belied his gruff tone. "It will take time, of course. Years and years of getting to know you." He chuckled. "And teaching you to love me as dearly as I love you."

Her eyes filled with tears. She darted her tongue against her mouth to moisten her lips and lifted her face in a beatific smile. "I think, my lord, that the lessons have long since begun."

EPILOGUE

IN THE DAYS THAT FOLLOWED the unmasking of Yvette Claudine Françoise Bouvier, all twelve of London's daily newspapers vied for personal interviews with the daughter of the once infamous Antoine Bouvier. At Andrew's suggestion, The Lark's Nest was temporarily closed and Yvette and Udora, complete with their household staff, removed to Valley Park, Andrew's seldom-used country home near Bath.

If Yvette had been popular before, after her noble birth and sensational background had been revealed, every eligible male under the age of seventy made certain to leave his calling card at The Lark's Nest. Making daily rounds to inspect the house, Andrew reluctantly relayed the messages to Yvette, but it was clear to her that he brooked no nonsense about them. Yvette was his. Their betrothal was accomplished. All that remained was for the general public to be made aware of it. Lady Bancroft was already submerged in preparations for the extravagant betrothal party which would take place in three weeks' time at Bancroft House.

It was she who had changed more than anyone else following that night at Marlborough House when Yvette had been assaulted by Clifford Waxton. Lady Bancroft had changed from a lioness protecting her cub, to a doting mother-in-law-to-be. She assured Yvette that, inasmuch as her lineage had proved to be acceptable, she had no objection to the betrothal. Indeed, she showered Yvette and Udora with so many gifts and so much attention that Udora remarked a bit ruefully that Lady Bancroft, the dragon, was scarcely a shade less wearing than Lady Bancroft the benevolent friend.

Driven to her wit's end by Lady Bancroft's smugness, Udora took it upon herself, one day at tea, to properly set her down.

"You do realize, of course, Lady Bancroft, that Andrew offered for Yvette even before the truth about her birth was revealed?"

Lady Bancroft put her cup down a little too quickly. "I do believe he mentioned something of the sort to me." She smiled. "One cannot fault his instincts, though, can one? It is plain to see that he recognized quality at the outset."

"Yes. Though I must say," Udora said naughtily, "isn't it strange that you lacked similar insight?"

Lady Bancroft swivelled her gaze from Udora to Yvette and back again. She blanched. "In truth, the problem lay in the fact that Yvette and I saw very little of each other. I trust we shall remedy that in the future."

Yvette was quick to assure her that she looked forward to getting to know her. She had mixed emotions about the little exchanges between Udora and Lady Bancroft. It was refreshing to see the pompous Lady Bancroft on the defensive, but she was, after all, Andrew's mother. For Andrew's sake they must keep peace in the family.

As the days blended one into another Yvette came to respect her future mother-in-law for her dedication to the family. It was through Lady Bancroft's determined efforts that Yvette's own family name was cleared. Once the amount of the gambling debt incurred by Archibald Wolgren was established, Lady Bancroft took it upon herself to see that the funds he had embezzled from the Poole

Shipping Company were repaid. He was, after all, a remote cousin. Never let it be said that there was any reason to cast shame upon the family name.

Clifford Waxton was charged and sent to gaol, but through the family's intervention he was soon released. He vowed that he would give a year of his life if he could atone for having wrongly placed the blame on Yvette's father.

Because the scandal had come to light during the ball at Marlborough House, it had proved impossible to keep the story within the family. The newspapers made the most of it for a few days but the murder on Fleet Street of a certain John McCumber, a member of Parliament, soon took precedence. Society drew a cloak of protection about Yvette the moment her betrothal was announced, for she was one of them now.

Andrew and Yvette were married in the formal garden at Bancroft House seven weeks after their betrothal had been first announced. She was an exquisite bride in her gown of spun silk encrusted with pearls and diamond chips. No one had grown used to seeing her with blond hair, but never did it attract more attention than on her wedding day. Lady Bancroft engaged the finest hairdresser in London to arrange it in a high crown studded with diamonds that glittered beneath a white veil. The veil itself was held in place by a diamond-and-pearl clip, a gift from Lady Bancroft which had belonged to her great grandmother.

After the Bancroft wedding Udora felt an odd sense of loss. True, her own betrothal party would take place immediately upon Yvette and Andrew's return from their honeymoon, but there was an emptiness within her that she could not quite define. Charles was a dear. He helped her remove back to The Lark's Nest, where she would take up residence until after her own wedding...whenever that would be. Despite the fact that Charles constantly pressed her to set a date, she inexplicably demurred.

The days drifted into weeks, the weeks into months. Yvette and Andrew had returned, Udora and Charles were betrothed, and Yvette was expecting her first child. A son, Lady Bancroft decreed. She would have it no other way.

London Society would sorely miss their Thursday night soirées, for despite the fact that Udora attempted to continue the entertainment, The Lark's Nest was not the same now that the Lark herself had flown.

In one final celebration before Yvette's confinement, The Lark's Nest was resplendent with light, music, and the company of happy people. Everyone was there to share the festivities.

There was one unexpected guest: a horseman from Coventry who brought with him a message from the past. It was a message that would change Udora's life forever.

But it was Yvette's night—Yvette's and Andrew's. As they whirled about the dance floor, he bent to whisper, "I told you I always got what I wanted, didn't I, my love?"

Her eyes glowing, Yvette looked up at him. "You did, *mon chéri,* you got what you wanted, and—" she leaned closer "—so did I."

Everyone loves a spring wedding, and this April, Harlequin cordially invites you to read the most romantic wedding book of the year.

With This Ring

ONE WEDDING—FOUR LOVE STORIES FROM OUR MOST DISTINGUISHED HARLEQUIN AUTHORS:

BETHANY CAMPBELL
BARBARA DELINSKY
BOBBY HUTCHINSON
ANN McALLISTER

The church is booked, the reception arranged and the invitations mailed. All Diane Bauer and Nick Granatelli have to do is walk down the aisle. Little do they realize that the most cherished day of their lives will spark so many romantic notions....

Available wherever Harlequin books are sold.

HARLEQUIN
Romance®

This May, travel to Egypt with Harlequin Romance's FIRST
CLASS title #3126, A FIRST TIME FOR EVERYTHING by
Jessica Steele.

A little excitement was what she wanted. So Josslyn's sudden
assignment to Egypt came as a delightful surprise. Pity she
couldn't say the same about her new boss.

Thane Addison was an overbearing, domineering slave driver.
And yet sometimes Joss got a glimpse of an entirely different
sort of personality beneath his arrogant exterior. It was
enough that Joss knew despite having to work for this brute of
a man, she wanted to stay.

Not that Thane seemed to care at all what his temporary
secretary thought about him. . . .

Take 4 bestselling love stories FREE

Plus get a FREE surprise gift!

HARLEQUIN
American Romance®

THE ROMANCE THAT STARTED IT ALL!

For Diane Bauer and Nick Granatelli, the walk down the aisle was a rocky road....

Don't miss the romantic prequel to WITH THIS RING—

I THEE WED
BY ANNE McALLISTER

Harlequin American Romance #387

Let Anne McAllister take you to Cambridge, Massachusetts, to the night when an innocent blind date brought a reluctant Diane Bauer and Nick Granatelli together. For Diane, a smoldering attraction like theirs had only one fate, one future—marriage. The hard part, she learned, was convincing her intended....

Watch for Anne McAllister's I THEE WED, available *now* from Harlequin American Romance.

ITW